Shelley Silas was born in Calcutta and grew up in north London. Her plays include *Calcutta Kosher* and *Falling*. Her work for Radio Four includes devising and co-writing a series of ten short plays, *The Magpie Stories*, adapting Hanan al-Shaykh's novel *Only in London* and co-adapting (with John Harvey) Paul Scott's *The Raj Quartet*. Her new play for Clean Break, *Mercy Fine*, premiered at The Door, Birmingham Rep in October and opens at the Southwark Playhouse in London in November 2005.

Praise for *12 Days*:

'The answer to at least one of your Christmas present dilemmas' *Heat*

'These playful tales are guaranteed to infect even the hardiest of scrooges with the Yuletide spirit' *She*

'Our only complaint is we want more than twelve!' *Family Circle*

12 Days

Stories inspired by
'The Twelve Days of Christmas'

Edited by
Shelley Silas

Virago

VIRAGO

First published in Great Britain in November 2004 by Virago Press
This paperback edition published in November 2005 by Virago Press
Reprinted 2005 (twice)

A CIP catalogue record for this book
is available from the British Library

ISBN 1 84408 101 X

Typeset in Sabon by M Rules
Printed and bound in Great Britain
by Clays Ltd, St Ives plc

Virago Press
An Imprint of
Time Warner Book Group UK
Brettenham House
Lancaster Place
London WC2E 7EN

www.virago.co.uk

To: Sally Bowden – thank you, Stanley.

Thanks also to mum and dad for tales of the little pink fairy, Leah for being there when I heard my first story, Wilf, Lily and Kizzie whose ears are always open and ready to listen. Big thanks to Stella for introducing me to all her friends, Antonia Hodgson and everyone at Virago for their enduring support, enthusiasm and confidence, and Veronique – blonde is best. And, of course, to the writers for saying yes.

On the twelfth day of Christmas
My true love gave to me

Twelve Drummers Drumming
Eleven Pipers Piping
Ten Lords a-Leaping
Nine Ladies Dancing

Eight Maids a-Milking
Seven Swans a-Swimming
Six Geese a-Laying
Five Gold Rings

Four Calling Birds
Three French Hens
Two Turtle-Doves
and
A Partridge in a Pear Tree

CONTENTS

FOREWORD

The idea for *12 Days* came to me while I was looking through a traditional picture book edition of 'The Twelve Days of Christmas'. I began to wonder what kinds of stories a group of contemporary writers would come up with if given a simple brief: pick a number from one to twelve and write anything you want based on the day you chose. Let your imagination stray. (Could I just say now that I didn't pick Five Gold Rings – a lot of people's favourite 'day' – it just worked out that way. I promise.)

I went online and found that there are a few different versions of the rhyme. How would I choose which order the stories should be in, without someone writing and telling me the order was wrong? Well, sometimes you just have to make a choice. Part of my research led me to a piece of writing that offers the origins of the rhyme. It's not just a catchy tune about presents given at Christmas. Some scholars believe that 'The Twelve Days of Christmas' was written in

England as a catechism song to help young Catholics learn the basic tenets of their faith. It was written at a time when being caught with anything that indicated a union to Catholicism could not only get you imprisoned, it could get you beheaded, or hanged, or hanged, drawn and quartered. And a Merry Christmas to you.

The song's gifts hold hidden meanings. The 'true love' referred to doesn't mean an earthly suitor but symbolises God. The 'me' who receives the presents refers to every baptised person. The Partridge in a Pear Tree is Jesus. Five Gold Rings refers to the first five books of the Old Testament – the Pentateuch or the Torah – which give the history of man's fall from grace. Six Geese a-Laying refers to the six days of creation. Interesting when you read these two stories.

As a Jew born in India with grandparents from Baghdad, Calcutta and Penang, I was also brought up to know the rhyme and to know about Christmas. The fact that it wasn't a festival I celebrated didn't mean that I wasn't aware of it – the Christmas celebration is as wide-ranging as the ancient midwinter festival it replaced, and all cultures welcome new light in the depths of winter.

With twelve committed writers, I knew there'd be some great ideas. Even so, I was delighted and astonished by the range and quality of the finished stories. From Marx and Engels, to the King of Spain's daughter, from South Africa to the South of France, from an antenatal class with a difference to a London crack den, the stories cover a huge range in style, genre and location. They are humorous, moving, clever, thrilling, breathtaking, romantic. They will make you smile, cry and make you laugh. The upside is that they prove that the short story is very much alive and well. The downside is that there are only twelve.

And remember – a book is for life, not just for Christmas, Hanukah, Diwali, Saturnalia, Kwanzaa . . .

Shelley Silas
September, 2004

A Partridge in a Pear Tree

Stella Duffy

When the King of Spain's daughter came to visit me she wore a gown of ivory brocade cut into with diamond lace. On her feet were calfskin shoes and she carried a fan carved from a single elephant tusk. The King of Spain's daughter travelled from Seville to Cordoba by foot, then by carriage to Madrid. She waited two hours at the airport there, bought a Stephen King novel and caught a connecting flight to Barcelona. Unfortunately she left the book – just three chapters in and already dog-eared – in the seat-back pocket on the plane. After a brief diversionary weekend in Sitges, lunch in Tarragona, supper in Girona, she travelled the coast road up to Perpignan. I did not know she was coming, but on the day she left, a week after the feast of the Assumption, I knew something was on its way. I felt it in the water, washed my hands in a porcelain bowl and the cool liquid was heavy with waiting.

I will come to you in the evening, orange blossom in my hair. I will take your hand and hold it to my breast, you will count the beats of my heart. We will never go astray. Daylight may be marred by fog or rain, the moon waxes and wanes, the earth spins on an elliptical axis so that even the rising sun appears to arrive from an altered direction, adjusting the angle of shine from summer to winter. But the Pole Star and the Southern Cross have marked us out. I'm coming. I'll need a cup of tea when I get there. And a good book.

I don't know how she found me. I know why she found me. The tree drew her, of course. Pear tree, not nut tree, no matter what they called it. I should know, I planted the seed. It drew them all, my little tree. Cousins and kings, councillors, counts, and the others too. Those that would steal it, take the harvest, smelt it down, make their own precious things. There are always people waiting to steal what they can, especially from something as generous as my little tree – those welcoming wide open branches. But these were my precious things, they would not be taken. Having planted the seed in the first place – one part organic compost to two parts peat and sand mix – I too was surprised when the tree began. I remember my fifth-form biology, I eat bean sprouts, I know what to watch for.

I know what to watch for. The lie of the land, sleight of hand, wedding band. Your ring finger is empty. I will fill it for you.

I watched the seed unfurl and grow. And keep growing. First the kitchen windowsill, then a gentle tempering to the outdoors, terracotta pot bubble-wrapped tight for chilly evenings; by spring the root and branches were strong enough for the ground. London clay, thick and cloying, seemed worth a try. The blossom arrived first. It was not as I had expected, almost too delicate. We had a warm spring this year, lucky spring, a late and easy Easter, four full moons packed into the first three months. I know about trees, fruit and nut. Have read up on them, our local library sees a lot of allotmenteers, books pock-marked by dirty fingers. Traditionally there should be two trees, male and female, for the promiscuous dancing bees. I had just the one. It wasn't meant to fruit so soon. But it did. How it did. Nutmeg and pear. Pear tree with a little added spice.

I agree with you. After all, if the tree blooms a pear, then surely the branch on which it sits is a pear tree? And pear wood is mine, always has been. Sacred to Athena, Hera, Vishnu-Narayana. (I looked it up online.) I am coming for it. For the gardener too and your rough dirt-working hands. I don't mind a hard journey. I do not believe it is better to travel than to arrive, at least not in second-class accommodation. But the approach is valuable, a time of preparation, consideration. I gather myself, the advent of arrival.

Unfortunately one of my neighbours, nosy woman, always chatting over the fence, became interested in the tree's progress. It is the curse of our London terraces – you think I live here because I actually enjoy a recreation of the fifties myth, street-party stories? I certainly do not. Sadly I do not have the wealth to garner anonymity and my interfering neighbour saw the shining leaves. I had tried to shield the heavy flowers from her spying eyes, the prying spies I knew she would tell, a full mouth of secrets dripping from the corner of her curling lips. I built a shed around the tree, open to summer light, closed against winter dark. Glass roofed, glass bricked, creosote-edged beams erected merely for the scent, my shed was a place of translucent light and slow growing ease. I am no DIY expert, B&Q is close to the seventh ring of hell for me, IKEA a Swedish prison. But I tried hard, worked harder and, in the end, I was pretty damn pleased with the result. There are people who enjoy the process of creation. Not me, my moment of satisfaction comes from having it all done and dusted. Ready. Waiting.

I dressed well for the journey, packed better for my arrival. We had some troubles on the way, problems both with transport and accommodation. You have to pre-book Travel Inns far in advance these days and I prefer not to give out my credit card details on the telephone if at all possible, I do not easily believe in strangers. Well, but not easily. Still, we managed. I wore the silk brocade, ivory. It creases least of all my gowns. The diamond cuts can be perilous though, the edges are carbon-dated and sharp. As long as I take care to move with precision my skin generally stays whole. And the calfskin slippers are very soft, easy to walk in. I have read the new suggestion that even short journeys can cause deep-vein thrombosis, it is best to take precautions. I dance in my slippers whenever possible. Airline stewards usually appreciate the gesture.

Summer took its time and the blossom turned to fruit, growing full and fatter by the day, weighing down the fine branches. There was so much interest I gave in eventually, took the neighbour's interference as an opportunity instead. I offered tickets at my front door, a glimpse of the silver and gold for a tenner. For many of them that was enough. I could still feel her in my waters, it was growing heavier by the day. I worried for the meter, thick sticky ticking through the massy wet. The bill from our beloved Thames Water would no doubt be excessive, and I'd stopped going to work to guard the tree. The universe was perilously close to giving up providing. My quarterly council tax was due as well, gate sales were good, but possibly not quite enough for Lambeth's exorbitance. And still I sat, in the cut-glass shed. I knew something was coming, someone. I trusted her to make it all better. I trusted my tree. It would not give its treasures up to just anyone, nor offer the fruit to any hand.

I wear a ring on my left hand. Daughter of Athena, the owl that watches from my ring finger itches in a straight line to my heart. Summer grows hotter and the central plains are arid. We travel on, further north. I trust you are worth my journey. (All journeys travel on trust.)

Late summer turned to autumn slipped into the harvest festival, full moon and she on her way.

I can smell you. Your spice scent dragged me up through France, the TGV faster still for my nose's demands. Silver nutmeg in a hot toddy, silver nutmeg mixed into smooth mashed potato, silver nutmeg grated on rice pudding. You will remove the ugly milk skin before I see it, I know you will. The comfort dishes of my desire have dragged me drugged with aroma through the Channel Tunnel. Just twenty minutes and a cheering group of schoolchildren to cross under water into the sceptred isle, I dance the aisle and smile on England. Aquitaine's Eleanor would have loved this. Though perhaps she was more of a cinnamon girl.

There is a pear too, you know. Juicy pear, ripe pear. An always-ripe pear. Never too hard, never too soft, just right little Goldilocks, this pear is always just right. It will not rot nor drop from the tree. Well, you wouldn't expect any less from a golden one, would you? Not gilded you understand, but actually, truly, properly gold. So why all the fuss about the silver nutmeg? There is also a glistening gleaming golden pear. That's a big deal too, isn't it? I tell you, Marco Polo, the spice route has a lot to answer for.

Slowing down now for the Kent countryside, hops picked, apples stored in cool barns. And then houses become clustered, back gardens open their faces to morning-tired commuters, the train steadies me forward to Waterloo winter and tube tickets and escalator and lift and change to overground train and then street and 45 bus and you. Your house. Your garden shed of glass. So this is it. I am come. I ring the bell.

The doorbell is ringing. I can hear it. My little tree can hear it too, the sap rises. Nutmeg and pear sing softly to themselves, ringing through their metal. She has arrived, our very own personal pronoun of what happens next. I was eager before, nervous but eager, now I am just scared. What if I don't like her? What if she doesn't like me? What if I don't matter and all the fuss is, yet again, only for the tree? The doorbell is ringing. I rise from my ripped yellow stool – its plastic coating once matched a fine fifties Formica table – and open the shed door. It has been raining. I've been in here since last light last night and now there are spider webs in my way. Picked out in individual wet droplets, crossing my path. The strung webs are pretty, in a modernist Christmas decoration, silver-and-plain-crystal-nothing-too-gaudy, kind of way. They are also a sticky nuisance as I walk back into the house, through the kitchen, down the hall to the front door, leaving a dozen homeless spiders behind me as I go. I'll say this for the King of Spain's daughter, she certainly knows how to ring a bell.

The door opens away from me and you are just as I expected. Tall and lean and the tanned skin of your face is fine-etched from the many hours of gardening and building work during the long summer. You are beautiful, but then I would not have expected less. The seed would not have pushed through the dirt unless it wanted to take a good look at you. I stand on your doorstep, looking over your shoulder into the hall. Your house is a little more suburban than I would have thought. That dado rail will have to go. And I'm not sure about the coir matting covering the stripped and sanded floorboards. I know they are appropriate for the area, your age and your social group, but isn't it rough on bare feet first thing in the morning? We shall see.

She was short. I knew she was short because I had to lower my eye level when I opened the door. For some reason I had expected a taller woman. Dark, with long hair and longer limbs. The flamenco dancer classic, I guess. Not that she wasn't beautiful. And the orange blossom was a good touch. She did have the long dark hair, dark skin, big round brown eyes – a young Susan Dey, after the braces and the faked piano playing, and many years before *LA Law* turned her blonde. I was a bit rubbish there, at the door, just staring. It's not every day I greet royalty on my doorstep. The Queen doesn't come south of the river all that often, can't get the cabs, I expect. I wasn't sure how to address her. Your highness. Your holiness. Darling.

You stand aside and I enter. I am used to a little more ceremony in welcome, but you will learn in time. I will teach you. I am a good teacher, have schooled both willing and unwilling pupils. Between us there is a shy glance, sly glance, and I note your dilating pupils. Mine too, I expect. We have both felt the strong desire stretching from here to my home, reaching halfway across this continent. As I journeyed closer our joint passion compacted, a black hole into which all wanting poured. My suitcases are piled beside your wheelie bin, you pay the porters from my Lulu Guinness purse, take the bags in your hands and then begin a stumble of uncertainty. Upstairs or downstairs, where is my lady's chamber? You are reticent and do not know which room to show me first. I lead the way, unerring sense of direction, up the stairs, first right and into the bathroom. No bidet, how English. I wash my travel-dirtied hands. Your water is heavy, isn't it? Is that what they mean by the limescale problem here? We will install filters. Next week. For now I take your builder's hands, gardener's hands, hold them in mine which are clean and a little wet still. There is a hardened blister just north of your lifeline. I will smooth that, soothe that, my tongue reaches for the scrape of rough skin. You are coy, slow, I hear an intake of breath and smile. There is time. How about a cup of tea?

She unpacked, I put the kettle on. I was just starting to worry that perhaps she'd want some girlie herbal tea and all I had were builder's bags, when she walked into the kitchen carrying a small wooden chest. She had changed, jeans and a T-shirt. But she still wore the calfskin slippers. Fair enough, that diamond lace looked dangerous. Lovely, but dangerous. She sat the chest on the kitchen table and showed it to me. It was well made, old. There were nine drawers, each one lined in silver with a different faintly scented selection of fine leaves. She took the pot from me – our fingers crossed again – and began to mix her brew. Half a teaspoon of this, a quarter of that, one full of another. Each one dropped into the pot, falling with a gentle shush. Then the boiling water and then the wait. Five minutes, she said. Long enough to take a good long look. I thought she meant the tree, opened the back door, pointed the way past the ripped and hanging webs. She did not follow. It was not yet time. She meant me, I was to be looked at. Inspected is not too fine a definition for the looking that began again with my hands, lingered on my forearms, dwelt on my shoulders and back and neck and then came to my face.

I want to see you. See what they do not see when they sweep past you and out to the little tree. I want to see the one who planted the seed.

She touched my eyelids and the delicate veined skin yearned to open for her. She ran the back of a smooth-buffed thumbnail across my eyelashes and each one blinked for her, severally and individually. She traced the print of her index finger along my eyebrows and down to the tired shadows of my long waiting – I knew for the first time the perfect circularity of my eye sockets. She lingered with the quiet wrinkles at the time-folded corners, laughter lines, worry lines, crying lines. I could have told her the content of each one. She did not ask. And then, finally, she licked the ball of her left little finger and brought her own liquid to my dry tear duct. It was a surprise and a relief. The tea was ready. We had a cup each. And chocolate bourbons. They were new to her. She ate five and a half.

When I kiss you the taste on your tongue is of these English biscuits. They are nice, plain. Later I will feed you on my food. When I lick your hand the flavour is of your garden, London clay and spiders' webs, clean and dirty at the same time. When you hold me I am nearly naked. For a woman used to boned corsets, wide dresses, heavy gowns, this T-shirt is flimsy and easily removed. (Remove it easily.) When we lie together on your kitchen floor I wonder in passing about the cleanliness, how recently this room was swept do you have a cleaner will you clean for me wash for me touch for me love for me. I wonder in passing and then you are passing over my body around my skin under my heart and I into you and you back to me and this is why I have come, why I am here, where I will come back to. You are easy, quiet, slow, ready. The wait was worth it, I hear the song of bending boughs from the shed at the bottom of your garden.

I'd never had sex with royalty before either. Fortunately the protocols weren't all that different. She was smooth and soft except just at the waistband where the diamond lace had cut into her, leaving a lattice of small scratches, light scabs for gently easing free. When we were done with the kissing and the turning and the laying and the wanting we went upstairs together to wash. I ran her a bath and she lay back into the water. It was heavy and held her close. I would have climbed in with her, but she said that would not be right. Not on a first date. I showered when she was finished, cleaned the tub and wiped it down. I pulled her long black hairs from the plug hole, dried, combed and plaited them. Put away the thin rope of hair in a heart-shaped music box left behind by my last lover.

You are storing me, shoring me up, just in case. There is no need. I'm staying now.

She said she was hungry again, that travelling always gave her an appetite and the airline food appeared to have become even worse since the imposition of further security checks.

I don't mind the security, really I don't, I appreciate both the necessity and the effort involved, but I am very disturbed by that whole plastic cutlery thing.

She said she needed flesh, meat, wanted to suck small bones. I offered a frozen chicken from the freezer, fish fingers maybe, but she had come prepared. Pulled enamel pots and aluminium pans from the Luis Vuitton, condiments and utensils from her handbag, and an *A–Z* from her pocket. The shops were all open for her, workmen left their waiting on this ordinary extraordinary day. Her presence keeps us all willing working. It's a good trick. No doubt explains her home town's impressively balanced budget. We went to Stockwell Road where she haggled with an elderly Portuguese man, two small boys watching in admiration. Walked Streatham High Street from Brixton Hill to the ice rink. Finally took a half-empty train to Borough Market and came home with our afternoon arms full of essential provisions. The birds are small and firm and clean. A fine white feather floats down as I open the gate.

(Came home? I like that.) I will make you Toledo partridge with dark chocolate sauce.

I eat the chocolate, she grates it into my hand, hard and bitter, it wakens the edges of my tongue. She needs one glass of dry white wine for the dish. We keep back a glass each for ourselves and pour the rest at the base of the tree. Moisture enough for a London winter.

According to the old man in the high street shop, this bird laid fifteen eggs in one day. She was one of his finest, will do well for Catalan-style partridge, ten garlic cloves fat and pink, two dozen onions, not one of them larger than the O of your open mouthed love.

She peels each onion carefully, stripping back the finest layer of dry brown skin and exposing white flesh membrane beneath. She starts with a pearl-handled knife handed down from mother to daughter, then discards it in favour of the new one I bought last week at the Co-op, two small paring knives for the price of just one. By the fifth tiny onion her dark eyes are streaming. I stand at her left and catch tears for the stock.

Jewish partridge, we call this one, though probably the Arabs gave us the nuts, certainly the Romans brought the garum, and the clay pot belonged to my mother and her grandmother before. The meat is sweet and strong, I think perhaps you are too. They say partridges mate for life. You are a gardener and I am a cook, this should work well.

Dish follows dish, tiny bones picked and licked and sucked and cleaned. We eat small and delicate morsels across a whole day. The postman comes and goes, local bin men collect carefully piled recycling bottles and paper, black liner bags stuffed with onion skins and greasy paper napkins. I am so full. Full of her and of the day and all these months of waiting for her to come.

You do the dishes. I want to watch your Queen's Speech. My mother asked me to check it out.

Tidied house, street lights on, it's time now. We go outside. I walk barefoot on to a frosted ground, it must be truly cold for the suburb-heated grass to turn winter-crisp. I show her the shed, switch on the external lights. She is suitably impressed and turns to smile at my neighbour peering from behind tired nets. My neighbour has the gall to wave. The King of Spain's daughter pokes out her tongue. Maybe we won't be sharing next door's Boxing Day sherry after all.

Your tree is beautiful. As it should be. You are beautiful. As you should be. I am beautiful. But you knew that.

We consider dessert. A fresh golden pear, rice pudding with lightly grated nutmeg. But we are full, she and I, not greedy. Sitting in the crystal palace of my shed, me and the King of Spain's daughter at my side, we talk of her journey and the heavy water of my knowing and if she thinks she will like Brussels sprouts. I use my father's sister's recipe, cook them with chunks of salty bacon and stir in double cream at the very last minute. It's really not bad. Above us, reaching up to the glass ceiling and the pale orange sky of this old city, hang a silver nutmeg, a golden pear, and the wishbone of a partridge in a pear tree. The little tree is good to lean against, solid. You tell me your studies: Athena was worshipped as the mother of all pear trees. Perdix, one of Athena's sacred kings, became the partridge when he died – but in Badrinath, in the Himalayas, he himself was the Lord of the Pear Trees.

This tree is male–female, it carries us all.

Everyone always talks about the partridge, don't they? As if that were the point being made, the lone partridge, waiting hungrily for his lifelong mate. No one really thinks about the tree, how the precious fruit would grow, where the bird would land if the tree wasn't there. But I do, I planted it.

You planted it. It called me to you.

And now it holds us up.

Two Turtle-Doves

Mike Gayle

1.57 p.m.

Crunching his way through the crisp snow along the pavement outside his destination, David came to a halt and looked at his watch. It was three minutes to two. He was pleased that he was on time for this, his final counselling appointment with his wife, Cathy and their relationship counsellor, Caroline. He thought it was a good sign. A sign that he had changed. As an act of rebellion the first time David had attended counselling with Cathy he deliberately tried to time his arrival at the centre for ten minutes after the session had begun. He thought he'd make more of an entrance that way and show both Cathy and Caroline who was boss. Unfortunately for him he completely misjudged how long it took to get to Crouch End and ended up being ten minutes early and as it was raining heavily he had no choice but to go inside immediately. He ended up sitting in the waiting room alone for a full five minutes before Cathy arrived.

As he walked up the snow-covered steps towards an Edwardian double-fronted terrace he looked up at the sign above the doorway. In large red letters against a white background it said: CROUCH END CENTRE FOR RELATIONSHIP COUNSELLING. David smiled to himself as he recalled how he'd shuddered involuntarily the first time Cathy had told him the name of this place and yet now here he was all these months later actually looking forward to being here, albeit for the last time. Before opening the door to the centre he looked into the window of the waiting room. Through the branches of the artificial Christmas tree covered in sparkling tinsel and adorned with flashing lights he could just about make out Cathy sitting on a chair reading a magazine. He stood and watched her for a moment and wondered if she looked any different. Did she look like a woman who had made one of the biggest decisions of her life?

Entering the waiting room he looked around briefly. It was still quite easy to imagine his surroundings as the Edwardian sitting room it had once been; the original coving and open fireplace were intact. Around the edge were a number of soft chairs and occasional tables covered with magazines and leaflets to help clients kill time. Week after week David and Cathy had sat on these very same chairs, at best making polite conversation, at worst glaring at each other frostily, and yet the moment they entered Caroline's office everything changed between them. They could talk. They could listen. They could express what it was they were really feeling. But in the waiting room it was different. Their feelings were bottled up. Fizzing away. Waiting for the designated time to be released with Caroline acting as referee.

Cathy looked up from her magazine and smiled at David, then mouthed a silent hello. She was wearing a beige overcoat done up to her chin, cream scarf, grey wide-legged trousers, and black boots with a slight heel. She looked well, all things considered. Her hair was just right, her make-up made her look as if she was glowing with vitality on this winter's evening, like an advertisement for the apple a day maxim.

David turned his attention to the receptionist. He'd never seen this one before. She was surrounded by the usual accoutrements: a telephone, a computer with anti-glare screen, a printer, an in tray and an out tray, a number of official looking files piled to her left. She almost seemed lost.

'Can I help you, sir?' she asked.

'I've got an appointment,' he replied. 'At two o'clock.'

She looked at her computer screen. 'Ah,' she replied reading from the screen. 'Here you are: Session with Caroline Roberts for a Mr and Mrs . . .' She looked at David and blinked several times as though adjusting her eyes and said,

'Turtle-Dove. Would you like to take a seat? Caroline is running a little late this afternoon. She's been out of the office all day on a course in Balham. She's on her way and she shouldn't be too long.'

David shrugged and with a sigh headed towards Cathy.

'David,' Cathy greeted him cheerily. She put down the magazine, and stood up as he approached. 'How are you? How have you been?'

'I'm fine,' he replied. 'And you?'

'Good, thanks.' She nodded a little too enthusiastically to make her point. 'Really good.'

'*Really good*?' asked David, his eyes searching her face.

Cathy shook her head vigorously as if to indicate that she hadn't been out partying every night. 'Well, not really *really* good,' she added. 'I don't think anyone's ever that good. But, you know, everyday ordinary kind of good.'

'Good,' said David as they both sat down. 'I'm glad that you're . . .' he paused as if unsure what to say next and looked at Cathy, who in turn looked down at her shoes. For a few moments a silence fell around them echoing the snow outside. 'That was a really stupid thing to say, wasn't it?' said David ineptly.

'Don't worry,' said Cathy, smiling awkwardly. 'It was fine.

'Have you finally decided what you're doing for Christmas?' she asked brightly.

'I'm going to drive up to see my folks in the morning,' said David. 'I'll only stay a few days. What about you?'

21

'Julia and Martin have invited me to theirs for a few days. And then I'll go and see Mum on the 28th. She'll be at my sister's until then so it all kind of works out.'

There was another long silence but David didn't feel compelled to speak. He was content to stare out of the window watching the snow brush silently against the window panes. Eventually Cathy reached into her bag, pulled out a novel and began reading. In response David stood up and walked over to a pile of magazines on a table in the corner of the room. He picked one off the top without looking and returned to his seat, only to find it was a three-year-old copy of *Bella*. With a barely audible sigh he opened up the pages and began reading.

2.11 p.m.

David was in the middle of an article about a woman whose husband ran off first with her mother and then with her younger sister when he realised that something was wrong. He looked at his watch. He caught the receptionist's eye and she immediately looked apologetic.

'I've just tried Caroline's mobile phone,' she explained, 'but it's gone straight through to her voicemail, I'm afraid. I've left a message and she knows you're waiting.'

David nodded and bit his lip nervously. This wasn't like Caroline at all. She was always a stickler for being on time. He nudged Cathy.

'This is odd, isn't it?' said David. 'Us sitting here, not saying much when we should be in Caroline's office baring our souls. I'm kind of half expecting Caroline to pop up from nowhere with her mumsy smile, large bosom and Scholl sandals and ask us to tell her something about our private lives.'

Cathy sniggered shyly, like a naughty schoolgirl whilst keeping her eye on the receptionist. 'I know what you mean,' she said, barely moving her lips.

2.17 p.m.

David put down the copy of *Homes and Gardens*. He had now flicked through several magazines covering a variety of topics from horse riding through to classic car maintenance and had decided he could read no more. He looked across at the receptionist who was now rummaging through a tall grey filing cabinet. As she returned to her chair she caught his eye once more. 'I'm ever so sorry about this,' she said. 'I tried her a few moments ago and I still keep getting her voicemail. Maybe the best thing to do would be to reschedule the appointment.'

'No, no, no,' said David firmly. 'We're fine waiting.' He looked over to Cathy for reassurance.

'He's right,' said Cathy. 'We'll wait just a little while longer if that's OK.'

David turned to Cathy. 'Good book?' he said pointing to the novel in her hand.

She shook her head. 'Not really.'

'I've never actually asked you this,' began David, his voice lowered to a volume he hoped would exclude the receptionist, 'but I've thought about it quite a few times when we've been sitting here—'

'Where?' interrupted Cathy.

'Well not here, exactly,' said David. 'In there,' he said pointing to a brass plaque on the far door which said: CAROLINE ROBERTS.

'What about in there?' asked Cathy.

'You know,' said David, 'I've thought about Caroline.'

'What about her?' asked Cathy.

'Well, you know, was she what you were expecting?'

'From a counsellor?' asked Cathy considering the question. 'Not really. In the beginning I couldn't get my head round the fact that she looked like . . . I don't know . . .'

'Somebody's mum?' suggested David.

'That's it,' said Cathy. 'That's it exactly. She does look like she ought to be somebody's mum.'

David laughed as his thoughts turned to his friend Nick, who had been best man at his wedding. 'Nick's mum has a touch of the Carolines about her,' he began, 'but I couldn't imagine sitting down once a week to tell her what a mess I'd made of my marriage – although I suspect that she probably wouldn't be averse to the idea. She was quite nosy like that.'

Cathy leaned in closer to David but not so close that it

could be construed as intimacy. 'Do you think she was listening all that time?' she asked. 'You know, when we were talking about us? Did you ever wonder if she was secretly thinking about what she was going to have for tea that night? You know, there's me and you talking about the problems in our marriage and she's sitting there thinking to herself, "Pork chops, string beans, carrots, boiled new potatoes and gravy?"'

'That would've been funny,' chuckled David. 'But if the truth be told I think she *was* listening to every word that we were saying – which is strange, don't you think? She must have heard our story – or stories like ours – a million times and there she is listening to us banging on.'

'I suppose,' said Cathy. 'What do you think her relationship is like with her husband?'

'Perfect. I think he gives her foot massages the moment she steps through the door.'

'I think you're right. I think he comes in from work and she pours him a small sherry before he sits down to read his evening newspaper in peace.'

'Do you think they ever argue?'

'Like we did? No. I can't imagine Caroline arguing about anything, can you? She's far too ... *personable*, don't you think? I can only imagine her being married to someone equally personable.'

'Do you think they still ... you know? Do the *horizontal shuffle*?'

Cathy laughed. 'David, she's probably only in her mid-fifties, of course they do.'

David paused to consider this before he responded. 'More than once a week?' he asked at last.

'No,' said Cathy shaking her head. 'Probably more like once a fortnight. I can imagine Caroline is into quality, not quantity.'

The phrase 'quality not quantity' made them laugh so much that the receptionist stopped her filing and gave them a look so stern it made it clear that she considered giggling inappropriate even if it was Christmas Eve.

2.25 p.m.

'It's getting ridiculous,' said Cathy to David. 'I was hoping to be back home by half-past three at the latest. I've still got loads of presents to wrap. Do you think Caroline's ever going to turn up?'

'Of course,' said David. 'Today's too important not to. I reckon she'll just give us half an hour extra free as a kind of an apology,' he added with a smile.

Cathy looked concerned. 'Have you got an extra half-hour's worth of stuff that you want to say?'

'Well no . . . not really . . .' said David stumbling over his words. 'But you never know, do you?' He paused. 'Have *you* got half an hour of extra stuff that you'd like to say?'

'I could talk to Caroline for days,' said Cathy breezily. 'I

26

really could. I think coming to see her was one of the best things we've ever done.'

'I'll admit she has been useful,' said David begrudgingly.

The phone on the receptionist's desk rang, grabbing both David and Cathy's attention. They stared at her in anticipation.

'Do you think it's Caroline?' whispered Cathy.

David smiled to himself before answering because after eleven sessions of counselling he no longer felt the need to answer Cathy's rhetorical questions.

'I think it might've been,' he said leaning back in his chair. 'But then again it could be one of the couples who come here for counselling . . . for instance that couple who were in the waiting room with us before the last session. Do you remember them? He had small beady eyes that made the rest of his features look out of proportion . . .'

'. . . and she was exceptionally well dressed and obviously so much older than him,' added Cathy. 'They were a really odd couple, weren't they? What do you think their problem was?'

'Other than being completely mismatched?' asked David. Cathy nodded. 'I think he thinks that she moans too much and she thinks that she doesn't moan enough.'

'Just like us, then?' said Cathy.

'Yeah,' said David but his answer lacked Cathy's levity. 'Just like us.'

2.29 p.m.

The receptionist put down the phone and looked at David and Cathy expectantly.

'That was Caroline,' she began. 'I'm afraid that she's still stuck in traffic and won't be able to get here for quite some time. She sends her most profuse apologies and said that she'll contact you to rearrange today's session.' There was a pause and she added, 'I'm ever so sorry about this.'

David sat bolt upright in his chair. 'Are you sure she's definitely not coming?' he asked, not bothering to hide the concern in his voice.

'Of course she's sure, David,' said Cathy calmly.

'But are you *sure* you're *sure*?' continued David. 'Only today's session was a very important one. I'm not actually sure it can wait until next week.'

'Oh, it won't be next week, I'm afraid,' said the receptionist.

'Next week's New Year's Eve, David,' Cathy reminded him.

'We'll be closed for a fortnight,' the receptionist explained. 'And Caroline's first couple of weeks in the New Year tend to be very busy.'

'What?' exclaimed David incredulously. 'Are you telling me there's a seasonal crisis for couples?'

The receptionist's eyes flitted from David to Cathy and then back to David warily before finally alighting on Cathy once again. Her look said: He belongs to you. Surely you should have him under control.

Cathy took a deep breath and then said, 'We'll just have to wait until she can see us, OK?'

'But I can't wait,' he replied. 'I've been waiting . . .' he paused and corrected himself '. . . I mean *we've* been waiting a long time for this. All the sessions we've been having have been building up to this point. The point where we finally decide if we're going to stay together . . . or break up for good. That's why this session was so important. We really can't wait any longer.'

'David, you're being ridiculous,' said Cathy, clenching her fists tightly. 'Another few weeks' wait won't kill either of us.'

'It *might* kill me,' said David sarcastically. He stopped and wiped his open hand across his face from his forehead to his chin, sighing as he did so. 'I'm not sure I can take the strain.' He stood up and walked over to the receptionist's desk. 'Look,' he began, 'I'm really sorry about this but is there any way you could contact Caroline to remind her how important this session is? Maybe you could give me her mobile number and I could call her myself?' David could see from the look on the receptionist's face that she was completely unmoved by his plea. 'But it's Christmas Eve,' he said, 'good will to all men and all that. Surely you can do something?'

'I'd really like to help you,' said the receptionist tersely, 'but I'm afraid I can't.'

'OK,' said David. 'I understand you can't give out personal information or anything like that. But can't she even give us a clue about what we were going to do this session? Surely she keeps notes or something.' David eyed a pile of manila folders on the desk. 'Have Cathy and I got a file? Maybe Caroline's written down something important inside it. Couldn't you possibly have a look?'

The receptionist quickly scooped up the files from the desk and clutched them to her chest as if David was going to make a lunge for them. Sensing that there was a strong possibility that the situation would get out of hand, Cathy stepped into the fray.

'She's not going to show us our files without Mrs Roberts's permission, is she?' she reasoned. 'That sort of thing's not allowed. We'll just have to go and, like she said, she'll call us and rearrange the session.'

'I don't understand,' said David. 'Why aren't you as keen to sort things out as I am?'

'I *am* keen to sort things out. Believe me I am but the fact is I've always been far more patient than you.'

'Fine. OK. Fine,' he said, which Cathy took to mean: *Not fine. Not OK. Not fine.* 'You're right. We should be patient.'

'Let's just sit down for a moment and work out what we're going to do,' said Cathy.

The receptionist coughed politely. David and Cathy looked at her.

'Er . . . I'm afraid we close at three today,' she replied.

'Oh,' said David.

'Of course,' said Cathy exchanging glances with David. 'It's Christmas Eve. Look, my husband and I need to talk. If only for a few minutes. We promise we'll be out of here by three o'clock at the latest.'

The couple returned to their seats and the receptionist nodded. Taking the files with her, she left the room leaving David and Cathy alone.

2.30 p.m.

'I've been thinking,' said David. 'Don't you find this all a little strange?'

'What's a little strange?' asked Cathy.

'That Caroline hasn't turned up because she's *stuck in traffic.*' He paused. 'Think about it: what if she isn't?'

'What do you mean, what if she isn't?'

'I don't know,' replied David furtively. 'Maybe she isn't stuck in traffic.'

'Why would the receptionist tell us a lie? What's to be gained by that?'

David looked around the room suspiciously as if checking it was safe to speak. 'Maybe we're being secretly filmed or something for one of those TV reality programmes? They can get cameras in all sorts of things these days.' He pointed to the receptionist's desk. 'That picture frame could have a tiny fibre-optic camera on us now.' He pointed to the wall to the left of them. 'That painting could be hiding a two-way mirror.' He looked all around them. 'In fact this entire room could be bugged with devices listening to our every word.'

Cathy shook her head in astonishment. 'And right now all they'd be hearing would be your gibberish. Will you listen to yourself? Caroline is a relationship counsellor – a middle-aged one at that – *not* a guerrilla-documentary maker.'

'OK, bear with me,' said David. 'Maybe we're not being filmed, but this could still be a test, couldn't it?'

'A test of what?' said Cathy. 'My patience?'

'No,' said David glossing over Cathy's sarcasm. 'A test of what we've learned. A test of our progress. How far we've come.' He paused and then said, 'Look, we've been coming here for ages now. And what's the main thing we've been doing during our sessions?'

'Is this a trick question?' asked Cathy.

'No,' replied David.

'OK,' said Cathy patiently, 'the answer to your question is: we've been talking.'

'Exactly,' said David.

'You've lost me,' sighed Cathy.

'Remember the first time we came here?' began David. 'It had been three months since I'd moved out and we were barely able to say a civil word to each other. Now look at us. We're making jokes. We're talking to each other . . . and here's my point. Caroline's not even here. Now call me crazy—'

'Oh, don't worry I will—'

'—but I think she's not turned up on purpose . . . so that we could talk. Just the two of us. Look at the evidence – she knows how much this final session means to us. And I don't know how she was with you but she even called me yesterday to remind me about this session and how important it was for me to be on time.'

'Actually,' said Cathy carefully, 'she did exactly the same with me. I thought it was odd at the time but . . .'

'See what I mean?' said David excitedly. 'She makes this big deal about us turning up and then doesn't turn up herself. Caroline's the type of person that plans for every eventuality. She'd never be late for anything.'

'You're right,' said Cathy. 'I remember her once saying that she hates being late for anything because she considers lateness a hostile gesture.'

'See what I mean,' said David. 'It's just too suspicious for words.'

Cathy chewed her lip, thinking over David's words. 'So what do you think she wants us to do?'

'I think she wants us to sort things out on our own,' said David without missing a beat. 'It's the one thing we've never done. Not really. Not properly. I think that this has been what all the sessions have been about – they've been about giving us the skills to sort out our problems on our own. I don't think she ever intended to have a final session. I think our final session is life.'

'But the receptionist is going to close the centre at three. We can't possibly sort things out now. That would be ridiculous.'

'Ridiculous?' said David. 'Or decisive? One way or another, Cathy, I think we should make the decision before we leave this room today. I really do.'

2.35 p.m.

'So?' said David.

'So?' echoed Cathy.

'Well?' said David.

'Well?' echoed Cathy.

'Look,' said David. 'Have you made your decision?'

Cathy nodded. 'Yes.' She turned her body a few degrees away from him before speaking. 'I . . . I don't think it's going to work between us again,' she said, looking at her shoes. 'I think it's over.'

David's face fell. 'Typical,' he snapped. 'Even when we're trying to sort things out we can't agree.'

2.36 p.m.

'You don't really think we should give it another go, do you?' asked Cathy incredulously.

David nodded.

'But why?' she implored.

'Why not?' retorted David. 'How could you possibly have come to the conclusion that you think we ought to split up?'

'And how could you possibly have come to the conclusion that you want to make a go of it after everything that we've been through?' said Cathy indignantly. 'I think the one thing I've realised in our sessions with Caroline is that I don't need to be with anyone to lead a happy, fulfilling life.'

'And the thing I've realised during counselling,' added David, 'is that we *are* meant to be together. I know we've had our ups and downs in the past, but the fact is we've survived them and I actually think it's made us stronger. You know, we work together. OK, we might not win any awards for lovey-dovey couple of the year but we work, Cathy. We really do.'

2.38 p.m.

'I know you're still in love with me,' said David. 'There's no point in denying it.'

Cathy's jaw dropped in shock. 'Why, you arrogant—'

'And there's no point in resorting to name-calling either,' said David. 'It's OK that you've been in love with me all this time. It's fine. And do you want to know why? It's because I think I was in love with you all this time.'

'You only *think* you were in love with me?'

'Well, I know I am now,' he expanded. 'But I have to

admit there were times since we split up when . . . I suppose there's no other way of putting this . . . I really did hate you.'

'And there were times when I *loathed* you,' snapped Cathy.

'And there were times when I really wanted – I changed want to wanted – to hurt you,' said David calmly.

Cathy narrowed her eyes. 'And there were times when I wanted to twist the knife in and give it *a really good shake around*.'

'It's a thin line between love and hate,' said David matter-of-factly. 'And I think that we proved just how thin it is. It's microscopic. Invisible to the naked eye . . . The truth is, though, there were times when we were arguing in Caroline's office when I just wanted to kiss you,' said David matter-of-factly.

Cathy shuffled uncomfortably in her seat. 'I never felt like that.'

'Yes you did,' said David. 'You must have done.'

'I'm telling you I didn't,' said Cathy quickly. 'Anyway . . . even if I did, it was only ever for a second or two.'

2.40 p.m.

'The fact remains,' said Cathy, 'I really don't think we can make a go of this, David. I think that the people we were and the people we are now are two different sets of people. People change.'

David nodded in agreement. 'Yes, people change. But they grow too, and that's what we never did until we started counselling. I think we've been growing and growing.'

'OK,' replied Cathy, 'so you think this is going to work. But surely it's only going to work if I agree with you, and the fact is I don't. These sessions with Caroline have helped me find out who I am and what I want from life and it just isn't you any more.'

2.42 p.m.

'So, what?' said David. 'You're just going to throw it away like that?'

'Like what?' echoed Cathy. 'Like you did?'

'Don't blame this all on me,' said David bluntly.

'I'm not blaming it all on you,' said Cathy. 'There were two of us in this relationship – at least for a while – and that was all it took to make things not work. But you have to admit that when I initially suggested seeing Caroline you weren't interested in saving our marriage at all.'

'Because I didn't think there was anything worth saving,' said David. 'We'd imploded. All there was left was bodies and carnage. I just thought it was best for both of us to walk away with whatever we could carry and begin again.'

'With Sarah?' interjected Cathy.

'Yes,' said David quietly. 'With Sarah. But to be truthful, Sarah could've been anyone.'

'How flattering,' said Cathy bitterly.

David shook his head. 'You know what I mean.'

Refusing to make eye contact, Cathy replied: 'Sadly I do.'

2.45 p.m.

'Look,' said David, playing with his wedding ring, 'answer this one question for me, will you?'

'No,' said Cathy. 'Because I know what it will be.'

'How can you possibly know?' asked David.

'Because after six years together I know how your mind works and you won't get me that way.'

'What way?' said David innocently.

Cathy tutted under her breath. 'David, you think you can argue me round to your point of view as if this is some sort of legalistic argument. This isn't a court case, it's my life. Just because I admit that I still love you doesn't set a legal precedent or mean that I have to follow the logic through or whatever it is that you're going to say.'

David's whole face lit up. 'So, you admit that you *are* still in love with me.'

'You're so infuriating sometimes!' exclaimed Cathy so loudly the receptionist didn't even bother to pretend she hadn't overheard in the next room. 'You haven't just caught me out with a slip of the tongue. There's no need to go: "Aha!" and point a finger at me as though you're on

Ally bloody *McBeal* or something. Of course I still love you. I've just said, "I admit that I still love you." But none of this changes the fact that I don't want to be with you.'

'You don't?' asked David.

'No, I don't,' she replied.

David shook his head in disbelief. 'Then why are you sitting here in this waiting room with me on Christmas Eve, of all days, arguing with me about staying together?'

2.51 p.m.

'Just think for a minute what would happen if we did get back together,' appealed David. 'We'd move back in together and just get on with our lives.'

'Would we?' said Cathy dismissively.

'Yes,' said David.

'And what about kids?' asked Cathy.

'I don't see why not,' replied David immediately.

'Now that's flattering,' said Cathy drily. 'You're practically telling me: "Oh, I'll try anything once."' She fiddled nervously with one of the buttons on her jacket. 'If you don't like fatherhood or you get bored I expect you'll just get up and walk away again, then?'

'What do you want me to say?' snapped David. 'That I want to be with you for the rest of my life? OK, *I want to be with you for the rest of my life.* And do you want me to say that I definitely one hundred per cent want to have kids?

Then, yes, I definitely one hundred per cent want to have kids with you.'

'I'm not asking for any of those things,' said Cathy. 'I'm just asking you what you see in the future for us. It's not me who wants us to get back together, it's you. I keep telling you that. The thing is you haven't thought any of this through, have you? If I agreed to give you and me another go this is what would happen: We'd move into a flat, we'd both be on our best behaviour for a month, maybe two, and then one day we'd be at the supermarket and you'd say something and then I'd think there was a "tone" in what you were saying and then you'd say something back that even if you didn't have a tone in your voice before would definitely have one this time and then I'd get upset and then you'd get upset and then we'd row or we'd not talk, and the cycle would continue. I don't want to spend my life being miserable – and you know what? I actually have too high a regard for you and the time we had together to want to make your life miserable in return.'

2.58 p.m.

'I'm really sorry,' said the receptionist, who was now standing by the door wearing a grey overcoat and holding two carrier bags in one hand and the keys to the building in the other, 'but I'm going to have to close now.'

'But we've got another two minutes,' whined David childishly. 'You said three o'clock.'

'Fine,' said the receptionist tersely. She returned to her seat at her desk. 'You've got two minutes exactly, starting from now.'

'Did you hear that?' said David. 'We've got two minutes left. Two minutes before we go our separate ways for good. Is this what you want?'

There was a long pause and then finally Cathy answered: 'I don't know.'

'You must know,' said David. 'You've just given me a big speech about how we're both making each other miserable.'

'I know,' said Cathy.

'And you've just said that you don't want to be with me.'

'I know,' said Cathy.

'So what exactly *don't* you know?' asked David finally.

'I didn't know it would be this difficult to say goodbye,' she replied. 'It's ridiculous but right now I feel like I could go either way.'

'Do you remember,' began David, 'I think it was during our third or fourth session, Caroline said that when people find it difficult to make up their minds nine times out of ten it's because there's not much in it either way – the pros and cons balance out on both sides.' He paused, and added, 'Maybe that's it. Maybe there's not much in it either way.'

'Maybe you're right,' said Cathy. She reached into her bag and pulled out her purse, opened it and pulled out a fifty pence piece and showed it to David. 'Heads or tails?'

'Don't be so ridiculous,' said David scornfully.

'I'm not being ridiculous,' said Cathy. 'I'm not being cruel. And I'm not being flippant either. The thing is, you're right. Christmas Eve or not, we just can't go on another day not knowing if we're going to be together or not. And if this helps us to make the decision then that can't be such a bad thing, can it?' David didn't reply. He just stared at the coin in Cathy's hand. 'What's it going to be? Tails we stay together, heads we split up?' David shrugged and shrank with embarrassment. From the corner of his eye he watched the receptionist stare at them in bemusement, as if they were some sort of avant-garde street theatre. 'We'll go with that,' continued Cathy and she handed the coin to David. 'I'll count to three, then you toss the coin and we'll leave it to fate. However it lands is the way that we go.' David nodded and Cathy began the countdown.

'One . . . two—'

'I think *you* should flip the coin,' said David, handing the coin to his wife. 'I'm sure I'll just jinx it.'

'Fine,' said Cathy. 'But I must warn you I've never been very good at flipping coins.' She took the coin from his hand and David began counting. When he reached three she flipped the coin in the air. Just as she was about to catch it on its descent the receptionist's patience finally ran out.

'Mr and Mrs Turtle-Dove,' she bellowed. 'I really must insist that you leave now.'

Cathy was so surprised by the receptionist's outburst that she completely missed the coin. It landed on the floor and rolled right across the room before it finally came to rest underneath the receptionist's desk. The receptionist bent down and picked up the coin.

David panicked and raced over to her. 'How did it land?' he asked. 'Was it heads or tails?'

The receptionist looked at the coin in her hand and then at David and Cathy in turn in disbelief. Without saying a word she handed the coin to David head side up.

'I can't believe it,' said David blankly. 'It's all over.'

Cathy reached out and took the coin, looked at David and smiled. 'Let's make it the best of three, shall we?'

Three French Hens

Annabel Giles

Christine had the distinct impression that everyone in the *boulangerie* was staring at her. Maybe it was because there weren't many tourists around in December. 'I'll have that last *pain au chocolat, s'il vous plaît.*' She was starving, it was lunchtime and she'd been too upset to eat the breakfast on the plane. 'Oh, and one of those little tart thingies too.'

She handed over her euro note, and the baker's face beamed back. It was an unusually forced grin, possibly the French version of the gurn. Did he remember her? Where was his pretty but arsey wife? Christine didn't wait to find out, she got back into the waiting taxi, and through mouthfuls of delicious pastry, began to direct the driver through picture-postcard Tourettes sur Loup and along the Z-bend mountain road to the holiday villa ghetto beyond. It wasn't until they'd driven too far to go back that she remembered she'd forgotten her change.

This morning had been a mad rush. When the line had gone dead, she'd headed for Heathrow immediately, and had just managed to get on the mid-morning flight by buying a Club Class ticket. But now that she was here, she wasn't sure why she'd come. What could she do? Despite the ever-present South of France sun, it was a chilly December day; but that wasn't why Christine shivered.

Julie realised she'd been standing at the kitchen sink for some time, staring out of the window at nothing in particular, although there was plenty to look at. The big space left by his car, for one thing. Which was now being filled by a local taxi.

A woman got out and took a moment for herself and her hair before walking towards the front door. Julie knew immediately that she wasn't French, she was English – she was wearing the uniform of her class, the pale pink pashmina set. This was the sort of woman who ends up in Peter Jones. Christine!

For the first time Julie noticed the dainty little mirror hanging just above the kitchen sink – how typically *chic*, she thought – but she didn't take a look as she wasn't feeling chic, she was feeling shit. Not sure how much more she could take today, Julie took a deep breath and opened the door.

'You must be the girlfriend,' said the blonde, without a smile. 'I'm the wife.'

They stood on the threshold, blinking at each other, taking in their differences. In the doorway was Julie: tall, naturally dark and prettier than handsome. On the doorstep, Christine: short, streaky blonde and meanly petite. Neither woman was much impressed by the other.

The taxi began to reverse back up the drive. 'I'll come in, shall I?' asked Christine.

'Oh, yes, sorry.'

Julie stood to one side as his ex-wife strode into the villa like she used to own the place, studying the hallway to make sure nothing had changed, acknowledging her satisfaction to the open-plan sitting room beyond.

'We were still married, you know,' she said, as if to justify her presence. 'We never got round to actually divorcing, but we're hardly likely to get back together again now, are we?' She laughed, a false-forced laugh, and ducked through into the kitchen.

Julie frowned as she followed. He'd claimed to be 'middle-aged, free and single', it was his funny joke, he'd always said it; and she'd been very pleased to hear it, every single time, she'd already wasted too much of her life on married men.

Christine opened the fridge door and stepped back at the smell. 'Good god – *Roquefort* pasta with pine nuts last night?' Julie nodded. 'Honestly, you'd think he'd have learned something new by now. My mother taught him that one. Aha!' She grabbed the bottle of wine from the fridge door and walked over to the right cupboard for wineglasses.

Our bottle of wine, thought Julie. That's ours. She'd perched up on the counter and chatted to him while he'd cooked their supper. Then they'd moved next door to the crackling glow of the hearthrug, and he'd tried to teach her chess while Norah Jones sang of jazzy love in smoochy blues. That was only last night. Their last night. Oh god.

'You cry away,' said Christine as she handed Julie her glass, 'get it all out. Use this.' And she handed Julie the kitchen roll, inappropriately cheerful now with its brightly coloured repetitive commands to have a *Joyeux Noël*! 'I'm just going to have a quick look round, OK?'

Nothing changes, thought Christine, with a certain amount of satisfaction. That revolting sofa was still in the sitting room – cream leatherette but wet-swimming-bum proof, peeling on the elbows, the orange sponge underneath showing through properly now. And Diana's armchair, incongruous as ever, straining to burst out of its ill-fitting floral cover designed for another chair entirely. Once-nice little antiquey table beside it, now ruined with too many rings from too many drinks. The doors of the cupboard under the black and white portable TV still didn't shut properly, Christine could see the yellowing sellotaped corners of Monopoly and Scrabble poking out from her past. Anonymous countryside scenes framed the walls, cheap ready-made curtains limply hung; grey-beige carpet Coca-Cola stained.

This room was a testament to the holiday home don't-give-them-the-nice-stuff-it'll-only-get-ruined mentality; so mean-spirited for one of the wealthiest families in Britain, whose London house was crammed with Important Pieces. But they didn't like to waste their money, which was probably why he'd hired one of the most expensive law firms in London to make sure he paid her the least possible maintenance. And that, thought Christine as she left to go upstairs, is how the rich stay rich.

He was perfect for me, sniffed Julie, downstairs in the kitchen, carefully dabbing the corners of her eyes. When the agency had described him as late thirties (and yes, definitely divorced), not many hobbies but 'very successful', pause, which was their polite code for stinking rich, she'd said wealth wasn't important to her.

But it certainly helped. She'd been thrilled when he'd invited her to his house in Nice for a short pre-Christmas treat (not knowing how jealous she'd been when he'd spent a week there without her just after they met, in September); and they'd flown First Class yesterday, all the air crew knew him, they were given lots of champagne and aromatherapy freebies, the full five-star treatment. And actually, she rather enjoyed her position back home as envied passenger in his Aston Martin, complete with personalised number plate. And he had a huge airy apartment, all beige and cream and genuine wooden floorboards, right in the heart of Hampstead village. Which she'd checked out that first Sunday morning, when he'd gone for the newspapers: bespoke suits hanging in the wardrobe, one of those plasma flat screen televisions and an expensively confusing music system; even his tea-spoons were solid silver. Yes, she could see herself fitting into his life very easily, thank you very much.

Another dollop of despondence dropped into her heart. She'd really fancied becoming Mrs Millionaire. She hadn't really fancied him, but he was growing on her. Even though he was her first properly bald boyfriend, he seemed to be a nice person and that was enough for her.

Upstairs, Christine's handbag rang. 'Where are you, Mummy?'

'I'm actually standing in your bedroom, darling, in France.'

'But I thought we were going to the pantomime tonight, just us . . .'

'Jackie will have to take you, I'm afraid.'

'Can't I go with Dad?'

Oh god. 'No, Phoebe, you can't.'

'But that's not fair, he's always working, and anyway I want to go with you, not my nanny, you never do anything with me, you're always too busy, it's not fair . . .'

Christine said 'Hello? Hello? Hello?' and cut herself off. Suddenly exhausted by the emergency of her day, she slumped down on to her daughter's little bed and clutched a heart-shaped *broderie anglaise* pillow to her bosom, by way of a hug.

Isn't it ironic, went the song in her head. In the beginning, she loved him for his distance, his difficulty, his disinterest. And yet that's what drove her away, in the end.

She wanted more for herself. He wanted less. She gave everything to her family, he gave everything to his work. She tried to entice him away with exotic holidays, he'd fly out for lunch. So she'd given up on him, and given in to Simon.

Who was passionate and adoring and sexy and everything her husband wasn't, and yet . . . She couldn't find that love again. She'd had it once and she'd given it away to a man who'd stolen it and kept it for himself and now it was dead.

Stop it! Christine stood up, smoothed down her skirt, straightened her hair. Got to keep going. Wonder if they've redecorated any of the guest bedrooms?

It's all right for her, thought Julie as she heard his ex-wife's footsteps overhead, she'd had the best of him. She'd had the chance to swan around as Somebody's Wife, buying crisp white linen trouser suits from local boutiques which she never got round to wearing, chumming up on all the right charity lunch committees, clogging up the narrow lanes of Hampstead doing the school run in the family 4x4. She'd had the lifestyle Julie wanted, and was damn well going to get.

She was working on it. The trouble is, they didn't have any history together, so she'd planned some for the future.

She was going to show him how funny and spontaneous she could be; she'd booked skydiving lessons for them, and a country Cotswold cottage weekend, and even a Saturday afternoon next summer in a hot air balloon. Her therapist had suggested she might be trying too hard, that relationships were better grown organically, whatever that meant. But Julie was fed up with being on her own, with living the loneliness of an independent woman. She wanted a husband, and she wanted some children, and she wanted them now.

Christine smiled when she saw the little bottle of massage oil on what used to be her side of the bed, and the travel candle in a tin, and the handy packet of Kleenex. Untouched, unlit, and unopened. Would it be really bad if she – ah yes, there it was in the top drawer, a predictable piece of silksatin underwear, lying forlornly in its tissue paper, waiting for some action. Christine closed the drawer again, horribly pleased that obviously sex still wasn't his thing.

Julie took her glass over to the kitchen sink and rinsed it out. She'd even planned a bit of a show for him tonight. She was going to seduce him, do a tempting striptease, make him succumb to her wicked ways. She'd never had to do that before, they'd always fancied her like mad, it hadn't been a problem. Actually, thank God she wasn't going to have to do that now, she'd been secretly dreading it.

A foreign telephone rang out, one long ring. And another. Christine stood at the top of the stairs, Julie in the kitchen doorway, both staring out into the hallway at the table too small for such technology, watching the phonefax ring. They exchanged glances, but neither moved, neither wanted to answer it.

So it kept on ringing, that one long ring, until the answer machine switched in. A pause, and then a lady with the voice of a dowager duchess on the piss said 'Hello, darling, are you there? It's Mummy, pick up the phone now . . .'

They stared at each other; still neither moved.

'Are you there?'

A pause, the length of a sip. A big sip.

'Darling? Hello?' Pause. 'No? Oh well, I'll try your mobile. Though I do hate doing that, it's so expensive.'

Christine tutted and leaned against the banisters.

Mummy was slurring a little. 'Have you said anything to her yet?'

The two women stared at each other. Her? Me? Or her?

Mummy went on. 'I can't remember when we decided was the best time to do it. Honestly, my memory's really going . . .'

There was another pause. You could almost hear the ice clinking in the glass.

'Anyway, listen darling, you're probably out having a nice time with whatsername, and – what *is* her name, actually?'

Julie tutted and leaned against the doorway.

'I really must write these things down.' She swallowed. 'But as long as you're all right, my darling, I don't really care about anything else. I do think you're doing the right thing, you know.'

Yet another pause, during which only the deafening silence of imaginations running wild and wilder could be heard.

'Sorry, not making much sense sweetheart. Not having a very good day. Your father's gorn orf to Venice again, with that trollop from—'

The answer machine cut her off with an elongated beep.

'So typical!' spat Christine, as she carried on down the stairs. 'She never made any sense. Have you met his mother?'

'Not yet,' replied Julie.

'I couldn't stand her. She's one of those people it's impossible to please, nobody is ever quite good enough for her, or her son. I'm sure she hated me. She was a terrible snob; so of course he was too. Did he check you out?'

'No, he didn't actually,' replied Julie, rather firmly. He had asked her lots of questions about her family, and education, but she'd naturally assumed that was because he was interested. Although, on their first date he did mention that a previous relationship hadn't worked out because she'd been *non sortable*. 'Not for public consumption,' he'd explained, 'the wrong class.' She'd understood that, of course, having stayed far too long in that relationship with her personal trainer.

'She's a total lush,' Christine continued. 'She'd hate you, you look far too clean-living.'

'Oh, I have my moments,' said Julie, not wanting to be boring, even though she spent a considerable amount of time and effort keeping herself in tip-top physical condition, which was boring. But she had to, she was still single. 'I'm just careful, that's all.'

'In fact . . .' Christine's face lit up. 'Come with me!' she ordered, as she brushed past and disappeared down the stairs into the basement. Julie had explored while she was waiting for him to come back this morning: the villa was much bigger than she'd originally thought. There was a fully stocked wine cellar down there, two more bedrooms, yet another bathroom, and a utility room. Christine opened the cupboard under the sink, reached behind all the French bleach and *canards du toilette* and pulled out a half-drunk bottle of Scotch.

'Good old Diana!' she said, triumphantly.

Christine went back up the stairs to the kitchen, Julie followed. 'Used to drive me mad,' she said. 'They were horribly close, always on the phone to each other, exchanging little secrets.' She reached up to the cupboard and took out a couple of tumblers which had undoubtedly come free with a litre of *essence*. 'Gave me the collywobbles, actually. Bit unhealthy.' She shuddered. 'I hate secretive people, don't you?'

He hasn't even mentioned his mother to me, thought Julie as she followed Christine into the sitting room. And I thought we told each other everything.

'I mean, I didn't find out for a number of years that this isn't even his villa, it belongs to his parents.'

'Really?' said Julie as she tried to settle herself into the armchair that was more uncomfortable than it looked.

'Oh yes. They've been coming here every summer since he was a boy, and because he's so bloody mean we had to keep coming here, year after year; he decided that it would have been wasteful to have paid to go anywhere else. He loved it here, I hated it. He used to come down on his own, to work, of course, for weeks at a time. Don't know how he could, this house gives me the creeps. And the chalet in Gstaad's not much better; every Christmas had to be spent there, of course. Very boring.'

It didn't sound boring to Julie, it sounded great.

'Drink up,' said Christine as she handed Julie her tumblerful of Scotch, 'you must be feeling dreadful.' She sat on the sofa, and began to pick at the peeling plastic, continuing something she'd started all those years ago.

'I'm just shocked, really,' replied Julie, grateful for the opportunity to talk about it. 'I still can't quite believe it's happened, it still hasn't sunk in. I mean, one minute I was waving him off to the village to the bakery . . .'

'The Daily Bread,' interjected Christine, wearily. 'I bet he said "I'm going to give you this day your Daily Bread, which makes me God ha-ha-ha", didn't he?'

'No,' said Julie, 'he didn't actually.' (He did. And she'd laughed.) 'Anyway, then I had a shower, and did the washing up, and made myself a cup of tea, and waited and waited for him to come back and next thing I know there's a gendarme on the doorstep.'

She shuddered at the memory. At first, she'd wished he was there; his fluent French would have been very useful. What with her *pigeon Français* and the policeman's pigeon English, the actual message had taken a while to get across, and the poor man had had to resort to a ghoulish mime at one point. He was ashen-faced, clearly unused to dealing with fatal car crashes in such a small village. Parking was more his *métier*.

He'd been clutching a shoe, by way of identification. And the baguette, still warm. She was told to stay here and wait, and then he'd gone, leaving her alone in somebody else's house, in somebody else's country, with just her feelings for company.

She'd burst into tears, of course. Typical. She'd finally, finally, found someone who was properly single, financially solvent, with no apparent addictions or sexual perversions, a man who would make a reasonably decent husband and father, and now he was dead. Honestly, how much bad luck could someone have in one life?

'Poor you,' said Christine, not altogether convincingly.

'Um, I don't mean to be rude or anything,' Julie took a tiny sip – she hated Scotch – 'but how come you're here?'

Christine threw back her drink, hoping the burn would detract from the pain. It didn't. 'He was on his mobile to me when it happened. He always rings me from the car at about seven o'clock in the morning, he knows I hate that time of day. But he can't quite leave me alone, you see.' She shook her head. 'Anyway, we were arguing about whose turn it was to have Phoebe for New Year, and then there was this almighty bang . . .'

She got up and walked over to the French windows, looked out at the blue-covered swimming pool, an inflatable dinosaur deflated in the cold corner, the life having been squeezed out of it.

'I can still hear it now. It was an awful noise, awful.' She shuddered. 'He knew he wasn't going to make it.' She moved away from the window. 'Damn, I think I'm going to cry.'

'I love her', he'd said, over and over again. 'Tell her I love her. She's the only one I've ever loved.' Christine could hardly believe it. 'Her', not me. She knew straight away who he'd meant. Although it was only because Phoebe had mentioned the woman's earrings left on the bedside table in his flat – oldest trick in the book – that she knew of Julie's existence at all, he'd hardly gone public about her. But this soggy blob in front of her now just didn't look like the sort of woman who could inspire such enormous passion in a man who couldn't even let himself enjoy sex. She was too – well, normal. Dull. I was his Big Love, surely – maybe he'd been confused, delirious. Yes, that was it.

The wife turned round to face the girlfriend. 'He kept

telling me he loved me,' she said. 'Over and over again.' She smiled, sympathetically. 'I'm sorry – this is probably not what you want to hear.'

'Oh, that's OK.' Julie managed to smile back. She was exhausted from the horribleness of it all. What a weird day, it just didn't seem real. First of all her future husband had died in a car crash; now his wife was sitting here drunk, full of tales of him being mean with his money, a total Mummy's boy, and still apparently in love with his ex-wife. But she would say that, wouldn't she?

It was all mad. She'd liked him, of course she had. But let's face it, he'd shown no real interest in her, he was more interested in what she could do for him. And the sex was crap and his jokes were awful. Was that really what she wanted for the rest of her life? She'd heard enough; perhaps his death had been a blessing after all. She was free now, free to find someone a bit more suitable, less complicated. Alive, even. Julie laughed; it was the laugh of a woman who realised she didn't care any more. 'Sorry,' she tried to cover her relief, 'must be the shock.'

There was a loud knock on the front door. 'That'll be the police, come to take me to identify the body,' said Julie. The horror of this task suddenly hit her. 'I don't think I can do it!'

'Course you can.' Christine had finished looking at the fading photographs in cheap frames on the mantelpiece, of graduations and picnics and marriages. She'd been edited out, she wasn't in any of them. 'Tell you what, I'll come with you, if you like. We can say goodbye to the old bastard together.'

'Oh, would you? Really?' asked Julie, who never thought she'd be so grateful to a first wife.

'Yes, might as well get it over and done with – then I won't have to go to the funeral!' Christine laughed; it was the laugh of a woman who'd forced herself not to care any more.

The policeman said it would be a long journey to the morgue, so Christine grabbed the French stick lying on the kitchen worktop, and some of the Gruyère from the fridge. Both women were to cry again, but not for him: for themselves, for their lost dreams and their broken promises.

As the police car sped through the village, the baker was shutting up shop. He sighed as he changed the sign on the door to *fermé*, pulled down the window blind for the night. What a day it had been. He stood at the bottom of the narrow medieval staircase and shouted up to his wife, 'Arlette! What are you doing up there? Why don't you come down and help me?' You can never trust a redhead, Maman had said, they're sly, like the fox. Ah, but love takes a man to mysterious places, he had told her. She had kept her silence after that.

Up in their bedroom, Arlette was carefully folding her favourite *chemisette*. She could still hear M. Dessaux's words, when he came rushing into the shop this morning to tell them the bad news. '*Il est mort! L'Anglais, il est mort!*' Of course she knew everyone's eyes would be on her, and so she continued serving Mme Cherruault, and even managed to exchange pleasantries with a few more customers until she could make an excuse to come upstairs. She'd stayed up here for the rest of the day, thinking between the tears about what to do next. The baker hadn't come after her; he knew when to leave her alone. Everybody in the village knew how she felt about *l'Anglais*.

She'd loved him since she was a child, you see, and she had made no secret of it. Right from the day she'd taken his shy little hand and shown him where the violets grew at the foot of the fortress, where you could hide in the hum of the weavers' looms, where the gorge was at its deepest point. They had spent all their days together, and eventually their nights too. They had kept each other's secrets, they lived in their own love. She knew him better than he knew himself.

Each year, when he had gone back to his own country after the long summer, one of the local boys would try to win her over – but they never could. Her body belonged to him and so did her heart.

Which he had broken into many pieces when she discovered that he had married. How could he pretend their passion didn't exist like this? But she didn't let him see how she hurt, of course not; in fact, she had even taken a husband of her own. The baker was a kind man, and he understood, but she felt little for him.

'Arlette!' came the cry from downstairs, '*ca va*?' Poor man, he sounded concerned.

She could feel the loss in her loins, in her bosom, in her arms, her legs, her whole being. She couldn't believe it had ended this way. Just this morning they had made love with their usual need for each other, but quickly and quietly; they could hear the baker joking with the clientele in the shop downstairs, pretending that he didn't know his wife was fucking another man upstairs.

'Arlette?' The affection in his voice was choking her.

'*Je viens, je viens!*' Arlette picked up her other pair of shoes from the bottom of the wooden wardrobe, and blew the dust off them. Her lover had wanted to talk after, but she couldn't wait any longer to tell her news. It was not as she had imagined. He had said nothing; but his face was shocked, and happy, and sad, and terrified all at once. Then he cried, and said he had come to finish their *affaire* for ever, he was going to marry again and didn't want his feelings for her to get in the way this time. He had forgotten to kiss her goodbye.

Que tu es stupide! Arlette chastised herself as she zipped up the tartan valise, the very same one she had arrived with on her wedding day. Why had she thought he would want to be with her now? She knew he could not love her out there in the world, he had never been free. Why had she thought this would make it any different? Now he had run out of time, and so had she.

61

Feeling a little dizzy, Arlette carefully stepped down the winding staircase and took her coat and hat off the peg. As she slowly did up the buttons, she felt the first stirrings of the new life in her womb, and smiled. *Ah oui*, I got you after all, *tu vois*?

The baker was sweeping the floor. He looked up, and began to protest at his wife going out at this time of—

'I'm leaving you,' she said. And she laughed; it was the laugh of a woman who had cared too much.

Four Calling Birds

Val McDermid

You want to know who to blame for what happened last Wednesday night down at the Roxette? Margaret Thatcher, that's who. Never mind the ones that actually did it. If the finger points at anybody, it should point straight at the Iron Lady. Even though her own body's turned against her now and silenced her, nobody should let pity stand in the way of holding her to account. She made whole communities despair, and when the weak are desperate, sometimes crime seems the easiest way out. Our Dickson says that's an argument that would never stand up in a court of law. But given how useless the police round here are, it's not likely to come to that.

You want to know why what happened last Wednesday

night at the Roxette happened at all? You have to go back twenty years. To the miners' strike. They teach it to the bairns now as history, but I lived through it and it's as sharp in my memory as yesterday. After she beat the Argies in the Falklands, Thatcher fell in love with the taste of victory, and the miners were her number one target. She was determined to break us, and she didn't care what it took. Arthur Scargill, the miners' leader, was as bloody-minded as she was, and when he called his men out on strike, my Alan walked out along with every other miner in his pit.

We all thought it would be over in a matter of weeks at the most. But no bugger would give an inch. Weeks turned into months, the seasons slipped from spring through summer and autumn into winter. We had four bairns to feed and not a penny coming in. Our savings went; then our insurance policies; and finally, my jewellery. We'd go to bed hungry and wake up the same way, our bellies rumbling like the slow grumble of the armoured police vans that regularly rolled round the streets of our town to remind us who we were fighting. Sometimes they'd taunt us by sitting in their vans flaunting their takeaways, even throwing half-eaten fish suppers out on the pavements as they drove by. Anything to rub our noses in the overtime they were coining by keeping us in our places.

We were desperate. I heard tell that some of the wives even went on the game, taking a bus down to the big cities for the day. But nobody from round our way sank that low.

Or not that I know of. But lives changed for ever during that long hellish year, mine among them.

It's a measure of how low we all sank that when I heard Mattie Barnard had taken a heart attack and died, my first thought wasn't for his widow. It was for his job. I think I got down the Roxette faster than the Co-op Funeral Service got to Mattie's. Tyson Herbert, the manager, hadn't even heard the news. But I didn't let that stop me. 'I want Mattie's job,' I told him, straight out while he was still reeling from the shock.

'Now hang on a minute, Noreen,' he said warily. He was always cautious, was Tyson Herbert. You could lose the will to live waiting for him to turn right at a junction. 'You know as well as I do that bingo calling is a man's job. It's always been that way. A touch of authority. Dicky bow and dinner jacket. The BBC might have let their standards slip, but here at the Roxette, we do things the right way.' Ponderous as a bloody elephant.

'That's against the law nowadays, Tyson,' I said. 'You cannot have rules like that any more. Only if you're a lavatory cleaner or something. And as far as I'm aware, cleaning the Gents wasn't part of Mattie's job.'

Well, we had a bit of a to and fro, but in the end, Tyson Herbert gave in. He didn't have a lot of choice. The first session of the day was due to start in half an hour, and he needed somebody up there doing two fat ladies and Maggie's den. Even if the person in question was wearing a blue nylon overall instead of a tuxedo.

And that was the start of it all. Now, nobody's ever accused me of being greedy, and besides, I still had a house to run as well as doing my share on the picket line with the other miners' wives. So within a couple of weeks, I'd persuaded Tyson Herbert that he needed to move with the times and make mine a jobshare. By the end of the month, I was splitting my shifts with Kathy, Liz and Jackie. The four calling birds, my Alan christened us. Morning, afternoon and evening, one or other of us would be up on the stage, mike in one hand, plucking balls out of the air with the other and keeping the flow of patter going. More importantly, we kept our four families going. We kept our kids on the straight and narrow.

It made a bit of a splash locally. There had never been women bingo callers in the North-East before. It had been as much a man's job as cutting coal. The local paper wrote an article about us, then the BBC turned up and did an interview with us for *Woman's Hour*. I suppose they were desperate for a story from up our way that wasn't all doom, gloom and picket lines. You should have seen Tyson Herbert preening himself, like he'd single-handedly burned every bra in the North-East.

The fuss soon died down, though the novelty value did bring in a lot of business. Women would come in minibuses from all around the area just to see the four calling birds. And we carried on with two little ducks and the key to the door like it was second nature. The years trickled past. The bairns grew up and found jobs, which was hard on Alan's pride. He's never worked since they closed the pit the year after the strike. There's no words for what it does to a man when he's dependent on his wife and bairns for the roof over his head and the food on his table.

To tell you the God's honest truth, there were days when it was a relief to get down the Roxette and get to work. We always had a laugh, even in the hardest of times. And there were hard times. When the doctors told Kathy the lump in her breast was going to kill her, we all felt the blow. But when she got too ill to work, we offered her shifts to her Julie. Tyson Herbert made some crack about hereditary peerages, but I told him to keep his nose out and count the takings.

All in all, nobody had any reason for complaint. That is, until Tyson Herbert decided it was time to retire. The bosses at Head Office didn't consult us about his replacement. Come to that, they didn't consult Tyson either. If they had, we'd never have ended up with Keith Corbett. Keith Cobra, as Julie rechristened him two days into his reign at the Roxette after he tried to grope her at the end of her evening shift. The nickname suited him. He was a poisonous reptile.

He even looked like a snake, with his narrow wedge of a face and his little dark eyes glittering. When his tongue flicked out to lick his thin lips, you expected it to have a fork at the end. On the third morning, he summoned the four of us to his office like he was God and it was judgment day.

'You've had a good run, ladies,' he began, without so much as a cup of tea and a digestive biscuit. 'But things are going to be changing round here. The Roxette is going to be the premier bingo outlet in the area, and that will be reflected in our public image. I'm giving you formal notice of redundancy.'

We were gobsmacked. It was Liz who found her voice first. 'You cannot do that,' she said. 'We've given no grounds for complaint.'

'And how can we be redundant?' I chipped in. 'Somebody has to call the numbers.'

Cobra gave a sly little smile. 'You're being replaced by new technology. A fully automated system. Like on the national lottery. The numbers will go up on a big screen and the computer will announce them.'

We couldn't believe our ears. Replacing us with a machine? 'The customers won't like it,' Julie said.

The Cobra shook his head. 'As long as they get their prizes, they wouldn't care if a talking monkey did the calling. Enjoy your last couple of weeks, ladies.' He turned away from us and started fiddling with his computer.

'You'll regret this,' Liz said defiantly.

'I don't think so,' he said, a sneer on his face. 'Oh, and another thing. This Children in Need night you're planning on Friday? Forget it. The Roxette is a business, not a charity. Friday night will be just like every other night.'

Well, that did it. We were even more outraged than we

were on our own behalf. We'd been doing the Children in Need benefit night for nine years. All the winners donated their prizes, and Tyson Herbert donated a third of the night's takings. It was a big sacrifice all round, but we knew what hardship was, and we all wanted to do our bit.

'You bastard,' Julie said.

The Cobra swung round and glared at her. 'Would you rather be fired for gross misconduct, Julie? Walk out the door with no money and no reference? Because that's exactly what'll happen if you don't keep a civil tongue in your head.'

We hustled Julie out before she could make things worse. We were all fit to be tied, but we couldn't see any way of stopping the Cobra. I broke the news to Alan that teatime. Our Dickson had dropped in too – he's an actor now, he's got a part in one of the soaps, and they'd been doing some location filming locally. I don't know who was more angry, Alan or Dickson. After their tea, the two of them went down to the club full of fighting talk. But I knew it was just talk. There was nothing we could do against the likes of the Cobra.

I was as surprised as anybody when I heard about the armed robbery.

I don't know why I took this job. Everybody knows the Roxette's nothing but trouble. It's never turned the profit it should. And those bloody women. They made Tyson

Herbert a laughing stock. But managers' jobs don't come up that often. Plus Head Office said they wanted the Roxette to become one of their flagship venues. And they wanted me to turn it around. Plus Margo's always on at me about Darren needing new this, new that, new the next thing. So how could I say no?

I knew as soon as I walked through the door it was going to be an uphill struggle. There was no sign of the new promo displays that Head Office was pushing throughout the chain. I eventually found them, still in their wrappers, in a cupboard in that pillock Herbert's office. I ask you, how can you drag a business into the twenty-first century if you're dealing with dinosaurs?

And the women. Everywhere, the women. You have to wonder what was going on in Herbert's head. It can't have been that he was dipping his wick, because they were all dogs. Apart from Julie. She was about the only one in the joint who didn't need surgical stockings. Not to mention plastic surgery. I might have considered keeping her on for a bit of light relief between houses. But she made it clear from the off that she had no fucking idea which side her bread was buttered. So she was for the chop like the rest of them.

I didn't hang about. I was right in there, making it clear who was in charge. I got the promo displays up on day one. Then I organised the delivery of the new computerised calling system. And that meant I could give the four calling birds the bullet sooner rather than later. That and knock *their stupid charity stunt on the head. I ask you, who throws their profits down the drain like that in this day and age?*

By the end of the first week, I was confident that I was all set. I had the decorators booked to bring the Roxette in line with the rest of the chain. Margo was pleased with the extra money in my wage packet, and even Darren had stopped whingeing.

I should have known better. I should have known it was all going too sweet. But not even in my wildest fucking nightmares could I have imagined how bad it could get.

By week two, I had my routines worked out. While the last house was in full swing, I'd do a cash collection from the front of house, the bar and the café. I'd bag it up in the office, ready for the bank in the morning, then put it in the safe overnight. And that's what I was doing on Wednesday night when the office door slammed open.

I looked up sharpish. I admit, I thought it was one of those bloody women come to do my head in. But it wasn't. At first, all I could take in was the barrel of a sawn-off shotgun, pointing straight at me. I nearly pissed myself. Instinctively I reached for the phone but the big fucker behind the gun just growled, 'Fucking leave it.' Then he kicked the door shut.

I dragged my eyes away from the gun and tried to get a look at him. But there wasn't much to see. Big black puffa jacket, jeans, black work boots. Baseball cap pulled down over his eyes, and a ski mask over the rest of his face. 'Keep your fucking mouth shut,' he said. He threw a black sports holdall towards me. 'Fill it up with the cash,' he said.

'I can't,' I said. 'It's in the safe. It's got a time lock.'

'Bollocks,' he said. He waved the gun at me, making me back up against the wall. What happened next was not what I expected. He grabbed the computer keyboard and pulled it across the desk. Then he turned the monitor round so it was facing him. With the hand that wasn't holding the gun, he did a few mouse clicks and then a bit of typing. I tried to edge out of his line of fire, but he wasn't having any. 'Fucking stand still,' he grunted.

Then he turned the screen back to face me and this time I nearly crapped myself. It was a live camera feed from my living room. Margo and Darren were huddled together on the sofa, eyes wide. Opposite them, his back to the camera, was another big fucker with a shotgun. The picture was a bit fuzzy and wobbly, but there was no mistake about it. Along the bottom of the picture, the seconds ticked away.

'My oppo's only a phone call away. Now are you going to fill the fucking holdall?' he demanded.

Well, I wasn't going to argue, was I? Not with my wife and kid facing a shooter. So I went to the safe. It hasn't got a time lock. Head Office wouldn't spend that kind of money. We're just told to say that to try and put off nutters like the big fucker who was facing me down in my own office. I was sweating so much my fingers were slipping off the keypad.

But I managed it at the second go, and I shovelled the bags of cash into his bag as fast as I could.

'Good boy,' he said when I'd finished.

I thought it was all over then. How wrong can you get?

'On your knees,' he ordered me. I didn't know what was going on. Part of me thought he was going to blow me away anyway. I was so fucking scared I could feel the tears in my eyes. I knew I was on the edge of losing it. Of begging him for my life. Only one thing stopped me. I just couldn't believe he was going to kill me. I mean, I know it happens. I know people get topped during robberies. But surely only if they put up a fight? And surely only when the robber is out of control? But this guy was totally calm. He could afford to be – his oppo's gun was still pointing straight at Margo and Darren.

So I fell to my knees.

Just thinking about what came next makes me retch. He dropped the gun to his side, at an angle so the barrel dug right into my gut. Then he unzipped his trousers and pulled out his cock. 'Suck my dick,' he said.

My head jerked back and I stared at him. I couldn't believe what I'd just heard. 'You what?'

'Suck my dick,' he said again, thrusting his hips towards me. His half-hard cock dangled in front of my face. It was the sickest thing I'd ever heard. It wasn't enough for this fucking pervert to terrorise my wife and kid and rob my safe. He wanted me to give him a blow job.

The gun jammed harder into me. 'Just fucking do it,' he said.

So I did.

He grabbed my hair and stopped me pulling back when I gagged. 'That's it. You know you want to,' he said softly, like this was something normal. Which it wasn't, not in any bloody sense.

It felt like it took a lifetime for him to come, but I suppose it was only a few minutes. When I felt his hot load hitting the back of my throat, I nearly bit his cock off in revulsion. But the gun in my chest and the thought of what might happen to Margo and Darren kept me inside the limits.

He stepped back, tucking himself away and zipping up. 'I enjoyed that,' he said.

I couldn't lift my head up. I felt sick to my stomach. And not just from what I'd swallowed either.

'Wait half an hour before you call the cops. We'll be watching, and if there's any funny business, your wife and kid get it. OK?' I nodded. I couldn't speak.

The last thing he did before he left was to help himself to the tape from the video surveillance system that is fed by the camera in my office. In a funny kind of way, I was almost relieved. I didn't want to think about that tape being played in the police station. Or in a courtroom, if it ever came to it.

So I did what I was told. I gave it thirty-five minutes, to be on the safe side. The police arrived like greased lightning. I thought things would get more normal then. Like The Bill or something. But it was my night for being well in the wrong. Because that's when things started to get seriously weird.

They'd sent a crew round to the house to check the robbers had kept their word and released Margo and Darren. They radioed back sounding pretty baffled. Turned out Margo was watching the telly and Darren was in his room playing computer games. According to them, that's what they'd been doing all evening. Apart from when Margo had been on the phone to her mate Cheryl. Which had been more or less exactly when I'd supposedly been watching them being held hostage.

That's when the cops started giving me some very fucking funny looks. The boss, a DI Golightly, definitely wasn't living up to his name. 'So how did chummy get in?' he demanded. 'There's no sign of forced entry at the back. And even though they were all eyes down inside the hall, I doubt they would have missed a six foot gunman walking through from the foyer.'

'I don't know,' I said. 'It should all have been locked up. The last person out would have been Liz Kirby. She called the session before the last one.'

By that time, they had the CCTV tapes of the car park. You could see the robber emerge from the shadows on the edge of the car park and walk up to the door. You couldn't see the gun, just the holdall. He opened the door without a moment's hesitation. So that fucking doozy Liz had left it unlocked.

'Looks like he walked straight in,' Golightly said. 'That was lucky for him, wasn't it?'

'I told you. It should have been locked. Look, I'm the victim here.'

He looked me up and down. 'So you say,' he said, sounding like he didn't believe a word of it. Then he wound the tape further back so we could see Liz leaving. And bugger me if she didn't turn round and lock the door behind her. 'How do you explain that?' he said.

All I could do was shrug helplessly.

He kept the digs and insinuations up for a while. He obviously thought there was a chance I was in it up to my eyeballs. But there was fuck all proof so he had to let me go in the end. It was gone four in the morning by the time I got home. Margo was well pissed off. Apparently half the crescent had been glued to their windows after the flashing blue lights had alerted them that there was something more interesting than Big Brother going on outside their own front doors. 'I was black affronted,' Margo kept repeating. 'My family's never had the police at their door.' Like mine were a bunch of hardened criminals.

I didn't sleep much. Every time I got near to dropping off, I got flashbacks of that sick bastard's cock. I've never so much as touched another man's dick, not even when I was a kid. I almost wished I'd let the sad sack of shite shoot me.

Everything I am, I owe to my mam. She taught me that I was as good as anybody else, that there was nothing I couldn't do if I wanted to. She also taught me the meaning of solidarity. Kick one, and we all limp. They should have that on the signs that tell drivers they're entering our town, right below the name of that Westphalian town we're twinned with.

So when she told me and my da what that prize prick Keith Corbett had planned for her and the other women at the Roxette, I was livid. And I was determined to do whatever I could to stop it happening. My mam and da have endured too bloody much already; they deserve not to have the rug pulled out from under them one more time.

After we'd had our tea, Da and I went down to the club. But I only stayed long enough to do some basic research. I had other fish to fry. I got on the mobile and arranged to meet up with Liz's daughters, Lauren and Shayla. Like me, they found a way out of the poverty trap that has our town between its teeth. They were always into computers, even at school. They both went to college and got qualifications in IT and now they run their own computer consultancy up in Newcastle. I had the germ of an idea, and I knew they'd help me make it a reality.

We met up in a nice little country pub over by Bishop Auckland. I told them what Corbett had in mind, and they were as angry as me. And when I laid out the bare bones of my plan, they were on board before I was half a dozen sentences into it. Right from the off, they were on side, coming up with their own ideas for making it even stronger and more foolproof.

It was Shayla who came up with the idea of getting Corbett to suck me off. At first, I was revolted. I thought it was grotesque. Over the top. Too cruel. I'll be honest. I've swung both ways in my time. Working in theatre and telly, there's plenty of opportunities to explore the wilder shores of experience. But having a bit of fun with somebody you fancy is a far cry from letting some sleaze like Corbett anywhere near your tackle.

'I'd never be able to get it up,' I protested.

They both laughed. 'You're a bloke,' Lauren said dismissively. 'And you're an actor. Just imagine he's Jennifer Aniston.'

'Or Brad Pitt,' Shayla giggled.

'I think even Olivier might have had problems with that,' I sighed, knowing I was outgunned and outnumbered. It was clear to me that now I'd brought them aboard, the two women were going to figure out a battle plan in which I was to be the foot soldier, the cannon fodder and the SAS, all rolled into one.

The first – and the most difficult – thing we had to do was to plant a fibre optic camera in Corbett's lounge. We tossed around various ideas, all of which were both complicated and risky. Finally, Lauren hit on the answer. 'His lad's about twelve, thirteen, isn't he?' she asked.

I nodded. 'So I heard down the club.'

'That's sorted then,' she said. 'I can get hold of some games that are at the beta-testing stage. We can knock up a letter telling Darren he's been chosen to test the games. Offer him a fee. Then I pick my moment, roll up at the house before he gets home. She's bound to invite me in and make me a cup of tea. I'll find somewhere to plant the camera and we're rolling.'

And that's exactly how it played out. Lauren got into the house, and while Margo Corbett was off making her a brew, she stuck the camera in the middle of a dried flower arrangement. Perfect.

The next phase was the most frustrating. We had to wait till we had the right set of pictures to make the scam work. For three nights, we filmed Corbett's living room, biting our nails, wondering how long it would take for mother and son to sit down together and watch something with enough dramatic tension. We cracked it on the Monday night, when Channel Five was showing a horror movie. Darren and Margo sat next to each other, huddling closer as the climaxes piled up.

Then it was Shayla's turn. She spent the rest of Monday night and most of Tuesday putting together the short digital film that we would use to make sure Corbett did what he was told. Lauren had already filmed me against a blue background waving around the replica sawn-off shotgun we'd used as a prop last series. It hadn't been hard to liberate it from the props store. They're incredibly sloppy, those guys. Shayla cut the images in so it looked like I was standing in

Corbett's living room threatening his nearest and dearest. I have to say, the end result was impressive and, more importantly, convincing.

Now we were ready. We chose Wednesday night to strike. Lauren had managed to get hold of her mam's keys and copied the one for the Roxette's back door. While the last session of the evening was in full swing, she'd slipped out and unlocked the door so I could walk straight in.

It all went better than I feared. You'd have thought Corbett was working from the same script, the way he caved in and did what he was told. And in spite of my fears, the girls had been right. My body didn't betray us.

I made my getaway without a problem and drove straight to Newcastle. Shayla got to work on the video, transferring it to digital, doing the edit and transferring it back to VHS tape again. I packed the money into a box and addressed it to Children in Need, ready to go in the post in the morning, then settled down to wait for Shayla.

The finished video was a masterpiece. We'd all been in Tyson Herbert's office for a drink at one time or another, so we knew where the video camera was. I'd been careful to keep my body between the camera and the gun for as much time as possible, which meant Shayla had been able to incorporate quite a lot of the original video. We had footage of Corbett packing the money into the holdall. Even better, we had the full blow job on tape without a single frame that showed the gun.

The final challenge was to deliver the video to Corbett without either the police or his wife knowing about it. In the end, we went for something we'd done on a stupid TV spy series I'd had a small part in a couple of years previously. We waited till he'd set off in the car, heading down the A1 towards our town. I followed him at a discreet distance then I called him on his mobile.

'Hello, Keith. This is your friend from last night.'

'You fucking cunt.'

'That's no way to speak to a man whose dick you've had in your mouth,' I said, going as menacing as I could manage. 'Listen to me. Three point four miles past the next exit, there's a lay-by. Pull over and take a look in the rubbish bin. You'll find something there that might interest you.' I cut the call and dialled Lauren. 'He's on his way,' I told her.

'OK, I'll make the drop.'

I came off the dual carriageway at the exit before the lay-by. I waited three minutes, then got back on the road. When I passed the lay-by, Corbett was standing by the bin, the padded envelope in his hand.

I sped past, then called him again a few minutes later. 'These are the edited highlights,' I told him. 'I'll call you in an hour when you've had a chance to check it out.'

He wasn't any happier when I made the call. 'You bastard,' he exploded. 'You total fucking bastard. You've made it look like we were in it together.'

'So we are, Keith,' I said calmly. 'You do something for me, and I won't send copies of the tape to the cops and your wife.'

'You blackmailing piece of shit,' he shouted.

'I'll take that as a yes, shall I?'

You could have knocked me down with a feather. I didn't know what to expect when I turned up that Thursday for work, but it wasn't what happened. I knew about the robbery by then – the whole town was agog. I thought the Cobra would be pretty shaken up, but I didn't expect a complete personality change.

Before I'd even got my coat off, he was in the staff room, all smiles and gritted teeth. 'Noreen,' he said. 'A word, please?'

'How are you feeling, Mr Corbett?' I asked. 'That must have been a terrible experience.'

He looked away, almost as if he was ashamed. 'I don't want to discuss it.' He cleared his throat. 'Noreen, I might have been a bit hasty the other day. I've come to realise how much of the atmosphere at the Roxette depends on you and the girls.'

I couldn't believe my ears. I couldn't think of a single word to say. I just stood there with my mouth open.

'So, if you'd be willing to stay on, I'd like to offer you your job back.'

'What about the other girls? Liz and Jackie and Julie?' I couldn't have accepted if they weren't in the deal.

He nodded, although it looked as if the movement gave him pain. 'All four of you. Full reinstatement.'

'That's very generous of you,' I managed to say. Though what I really wanted was to ask him if he'd taken a blow to the head during the robbery.

He grimaced, his tight little face closed as a pithead. 'And if you still want to do the Children in Need night, we could make it next Friday,' he added, each word sounding like it was choked out of him.

'Thank you,' I said. I took a quick look out of the window to see if there were any pigs flying past, but no. Whatever had happened inside the Cobra's head, the rest of the world seemed to be going on as normal.

And he was as good as his word. I don't know what changed his mind, but the four calling birds are back behind the balls at the Roxette. I still can't quite believe it, but as our Dickson reminded me, I've always said there's good in everybody. Sometimes, you just have to dig deep to find it.

Five Gold Rings

Shelley Silas

There was nothing unusual about the day. Saleem woke at ten minutes to three, a couple of hours before the sun was fully risen. He rolled off the bed, a thick mattress laid across the floor, stretched his arms high, reached a bit further so his fingers kissed above his body then dropped them to his side. He eased his head around in little circles, extended his legs, first the left then the right, gently pressing down, a few slight movements to loosen his limbs and waken his muscles. He had been doing this for thirty-five years, and somehow the day was incomplete without his morning ritual.

A turmeric glow from a street lamp spilled through the fine curtains. An imperfect moon hung in a cloudless sky. Most of the town was asleep, except Saleem. In other parts of the land, lovers and losers were returning home from clubs and bars and the houses of friends. And here was Saleem, wide awake.

He made a pot of strong coffee with cardamom, like his father had taught him. On the way to work he would buy fresh bread from his friend on the corner of Beit Sahur Street. Saleem jigged his shoulders up and down, glanced adoringly at his wife, still asleep, her rotund body covered by a thin duvet, her bottom lip quivering, her mouth emitting short snorts which he found endearing and she found embarrassing.

She was sixty-two to his sixty-one, short to his tall, fat to his thin, chaotic to his ordered, drunk to his sober, straight backed to his crescent-shaped spine. She was everything he was not. But they shared a deep love for each other, and this was what kept him from straying and kept her staying.

He'd listened to the weather forecast the night before on a radio he'd bought in the market in Jerusalem. They didn't have a television. When the last one stopped working they didn't bother to invest in a newer model. The kids had left home and Saleem and Mrs Saleem, as he affectionately called her, would rather spend their spare time talking and reminiscing than watching programmes that did little to lighten their mood. The radio had promised blue skies, constant sunshine, no sign of even the most gentle of breezes. The weatherman had been adamant.

Saleem peered out of the window. Everything was still and silent. The kind of quiet that always made him feel something bad was about to happen, not necessarily to him, but nevertheless, it was going to happen. Last time he felt like this, a few years ago, his cousin's son's wife had been stopped on her way to hospital to give birth. Not because anything was wrong, but because their car had hit a patch of particularly sharp gravel and punctured not one, but two tyres. His cousin's son's wife regarded this as an omen – she was a superstitious woman – a good omen and so refused to go any further. They asked for a ride from a cherubic boy with Ray-Ban eyes, wearing a uniform they had seen too much of in recent years. He refused to let them pass, said he had to wait for his commander and didn't offer any help when she explained her situation. He said she didn't look very pregnant and palmed her off with a sip of water, too warm for her liking. When her waters broke all over his army feet, he believed her, but it was too late to take her to hospital, so she ended up giving birth on the roadside, while dirt and dust swirled around. She yelled loudly and out he swam, a healthy boy with a bulletproof helmet of dark hair. Then the soldier drove them to hospital in his Jeep with the bouncy seats and empty food containers on the floor, and hooted his horn loud and long to ensure no obstructions blocked their way. When it was time to say goodbye, he gave them an unopened packet of cigarettes and a smile they would remember until the sea turned to desert and the desert turned to ice. Smiles like his were rare. They would remember that as well.

Saleem shook his head. He thought of his friend Avraham, in Beit-Hakerem, Jerusalem. Avraham's father used to drive buses across the border. In the days when curious tourists had little to fear, he would bring people from all over the world to visit the church. Avraham had travelled with him a few times. Perched at the front of the bus, Avraham's English was more coherent than his father's, his sense of humour more humorous. When Saleem and Avraham met – in Manger Square for a smoke – they knew they would be friends. Was there such a thing, they had said, as falling in friendship? Their trust grew deep, their families had lunch together once, but opinions were strained and apart from letters, the men met twice a year, to exchange deepening wrinkles and news and ensure their trust never waned. Saleem had a feeling it was Avraham's birthday soon. He would buy a card for him later – or better still make one, more personal he thought, and of course less expensive.

Saleem was a good man. He was proud of his family, his three sons and one daughter, all working hard although he hardly saw his eldest son and when he did, he was told not to ask too many questions. Saleem's eighty-five-year-old mother lived alone in a small house overlooking the hills. She rarely left her home, preferring to cook in her own kitchen, with pictures of her grandchildren alongside rusty utensils and a fading black-and-white picture of her wedding day. She visited her husband's graveside three times a year – on their anniversary, on his birthday and at Christmas, when she took a wreath of green and red and lit one candle. When she did leave home she ensured she had all her valuables with her, just in case she returned to a home with squatters or worse still, no home, just a pile of rubble.

Mrs Saleem woke to the smell of fresh coffee, bringing her out of an exceptionally good dream. She was on a yacht in the cool blue Mediterranean with young boys running around, showing her fat fish caught in the clear water, cooked on charcoal, with garlic and lemon. Her body was a size smaller, her hair blonde, not peppered with salt. She wore bright red lipstick and not much else. Saleem had appeared in her dream, his body fitter than it was now, short shorts revealing the horizon where olive and brown flesh met. Then his coffee permeated her sleepy vision, making her turn over and roll off the mattress straight on to the cold marble floor. She patted her bottom, sighed heavily. She would return to sleep once he had gone. It seemed impolite to close her eyes now she was awake.

Saleem and Mrs Saleem tended not to speak much in the mornings. The odd 'hello', 'nice weather', 'shall I bring something tasty on my way home from work?' accompanied their movements; his urgent, hers slothful. Occasionally she would bemoan the state of affairs, as her mother had done since 1948, when Mrs Saleem was six and still counting. Now she counted the wars and he counted the losses.

Washing was such a bore: often Saleem would squirt pungent liquid to his underarms, wash his face with quick movements, shuffle his feet in talcum powder and apply water to his lower regions. His middle son had bought him purple-coloured aftershave, which remained in its square bottle, unopened. Somewhere in his mind, he had decided that taking a shower was like taking his soul. So he preferred not to wash.

Mrs Saleem ensured he had a flask of strong mint tea to take to work, one apple and one orange – his cholesterol was high, his blood sugar verging on too much and his blood pressure, that was another cause for concern – yesterday's salad, home-made cheese and a bottle of water. She sat with her legs wide apart, the old blue nightie she slept in creeping towards the top part of her thighs. A yawn climbed out of her mouth, big and strong, lasting long enough for Saleem to take a picture. He had been given a camera for his birthday, a third-hand Canon that some of his friends had clubbed together to buy. And now he was making an album, a secret album, for his wife's birthday next week. He'd taken pictures of all the places they'd been to as childhood sweethearts; the church where they were married, the children, his work, the almond tree they had planted together, even the first teapot they bought in Jerusalem, which now stood chipped and ageing on the top shelf of their kitchen cupboard. He had wanted to throw it away. She had not. And so it stayed. The teapot, he thought, would be on the first page of the album. All he had to do now was buy an album. Saleem was usually more organised than this. Perhaps today, he thought, I will find one, and rolled a collection of coins from the table into his pocket.

She didn't look at him as he left the house, sat with her eyes half closed, waiting for the door to shut. He looked at her, smiled, whispered, I Love You and slipped out so quietly, he knew she would have to open her eyes to ensure he had gone.

The walk to work took twenty minutes depending on which route he took, which shoes he was wearing, the weather and his need to hurry. Saleem checked his watch. Daylight wasn't too far away. Soon, a ripe globe would rise quickly in the east. His bag of lunch swung by his side, his feet quickstepped, his back was slightly arched, a bow waiting to be released. As he grew older he grew thinner, like a tree in a state of perpetual autumn.

'Saleem,' his friend Yusuf called out.

Saleem nodded, waved briskly to the wizened old man with only one working eye, and a stall on the street corner stacked with bread. Saleem took out his camera and pointed it at Yusuf. Yusuf instantly showed his teeth, a picket fence neither white nor whole. The few he had were yellow from tobacco and tannin. He liked tea, especially PG Tips, which his brother sent twice a year from abroad. Saleem pressed down gently. A flash went off. Saleem nodded approval and cleared his throat. He eyed the bread. Large flat pieces. He took one, then another. He was hungrier than usual this morning. He gave the bread to Yusuf to put into a plastic bag with a little wrap of zahtar. He loved the mix of dried thyme, toasted sesame seeds, and ground sumac. Occasionally he would add some salt. He kept a small bottle of olive oil at work. Later, he would lay out the bread, drizzle some oil on to the centre and sprinkle zahtar all over it. Then he would roll it up and eat it with intermittent sips of Mrs Saleem's mint tea, although he preferred coffee. But Mrs Saleem had warned him that if he didn't take care he would die young, like his father.

Yusuf shook his head at Saleem. 'Why don't they all just stop?' Yusuf said. 'We must start to trust again.' He looked at Saleem. 'We must learn how to trust one another. Without that we have nothing.'

Another suicide bomber had blown himself up in a café by the water. More concrete was going up to keep them out. Or was it to keep them in? Yusuf was never quite sure. People were leaving, jobs were scarce and although it was only April, it had already been decided there would be no Christmas celebrations this year. Saleem thought they should forget about history and geography and start again. Yusuf drew a map in the air. Yours. Mine. Simple. Saleem corrected him. Yours. Ours. The problem, Saleem said, was that everyone wants more. If people wanted less, we would be all right. While Yusuf was hope-less, Saleem was hopeful, and here their minds parted, 'like two roads created from one', Yusuf said. Saleem argued that 'instead of creating a new road from the old road they should create two entirely new roads'. Yusuf was confused, what was all this talk about roads? Yusuf teased his friend about his thinning hair and thinning mind as Saleem made his way to work.

The almonds were ripening on the trees, ready to pick in June and July. Saleem passed the boys' school and crossed into Manger Square. He looked up at the church and felt safe. Being the bell ringer at the most famous church in the world was pretty special, though he wasn't so much the bell ringer as the bell presser. And today was no different from any other day. It wasn't a special occasion, there were no weddings, funerals or festivals. It was just an ordinary day like most others.

Except that it wasn't.

Saleem let himself into the church, bending because the entrance was so low. His eyes had never become accustomed to the change in light, nor his skin to the sudden drop in temperature from the cool brick interior. Saints saluted him as he walked by. He blessed himself with holy water and stood still for a few moments, head bowed in silent contemplation. This was his favourite time of day, when no one else was around. Soon, Father George would appear, but for now, he was alone. Here, he could hold history in his hands every day, breathe the past, feel it move between his fingers. Here he believed the impossible was possible.

When he was younger, when the church was easier to reach, the roads not blocked, the faces friendlier on both sides of the fence, his future more stable, Saleem would go up to the roof of the church and look down at the houses and buildings. Bells rang out from the Catholic, Greek Orthodox and Armenian towers, some at different times, at other times all together in one great confusion of sound. Saleem would stand and look out and wave at people, as if he were on the top of the world. Then, he had plans to build his own house on a particular piece of land, with a large garden for his wife and a garage for his car. He wanted a convertible, with power steering and a drink holder for his can of Coke. Now, he couldn't afford a car, and his plot of land already had a house on it, with a balcony and garage and someone else's Ford Escort in the drive.

Saleem's voice echoed around the cavernous church, as he prepared for the first ring of the day. It would sound at exactly four o'clock. The second would be in an hour and a half. At half-past two he would sound the final ring of the day. Saleem liked to think that all of Bethlehem could hear the noise he created by the single push of a button in the sacristy.

Before it had been modernised, Saleem used to ring the bell himself. The skin on his hands had grown thick from the pull of the ropes. As a younger man, he had refused to wear gloves, refused to treat his hands with the lotions and potions Mrs Saleem begged him to use. No amount of time could heal his wounds. He liked his hands, was proud of the scars that came with his work. They were often a talking point, especially with strangers. They would look at him, and then at his hands, at the hard skin creating a mosaic across his flesh, and stare in wonder, until Saleem sated their curiosity by telling them he was the bell ringer at the most famous church in the world. Of course people rarely believed him, but when they did, Saleem felt as if they had been touched by magic. And if they had, then he had too. And all the pulling and pressing had been worth while.

Mrs Saleem relaxed as she heard the sound of the bells from her bed. It made her feel safe, to know Saleem had reached work with no distractions. She slipped back under the duvet with her morning coffee, a fat piece of bread and white cheese, and a book, a crime story by a young English girl, a hardback Saleem had found abandoned at the church. He had deposited it in the lost property, waited for two weeks, and when no one had claimed it, he took it home. He had accumulated a variety of objects in this way, objects they would normally be unable to afford. Mrs Saleem turned the pages. She didn't really like crime, she liked the settings, the faraway places that she could only dream of. She was born in Bethlehem and had been away only a few times. Once to go to the Dead Sea, but there was too much salt and the only things that came away transformed were her abrasions. They had been to Solomon's Pools, on picnics many years ago, when the children were small and life was more hopeful, when looking over your shoulder was a rarity, and the sound of gunfire was a surprise rather than an expectation. These days they didn't venture very far. She hoped that one day she and Saleem would travel together, and he could listen to bells in other countries: Moscow, London, Paris and even Rome. Perhaps the Pope would allow him to ring the bells at St Peter's. She had seen the Pope on her neighbour's television, crumpled and pinched, half man half ghost. Mrs Saleem was secretly saving what money she could earn in an old copper tin, hiding it behind a loose brick in the walled yard her husband called a garden and she called a dead place where nothing grew. She hadn't managed to put aside much; unemployment was high, and she was one of the unlucky ones. But she was determined that one day, one day she would surprise Saleem with a ticket and a bed and breakfast in a town with a name he couldn't even pronounce and food that arrived on a tray and was carried to a bed raised off the ground.

Saleem remembered the pictures he had taken. A child, kneeling down. A nun at prayer. A man, glasses resting on the top of his head. A camel, a donkey, a cat and a dog. He realised he had no pictures of himself, and turned the camera towards his face. He clicked. Clicked again. Three, four times. Each with a new expression. Laughing. Pensive. Uncertain. Eyes closed. He hoped he was in focus.

During his thirty years at the church, Saleem had conversed with tall men from Sweden, short men from Italy, slim women from France, blonde women from Russia, garrulous groups from Australia. Between his three daily sojourns to the sacristy, he talked to them. They all came with inquisitive minds and digital cameras, videos to take moving images of where the great birth had taken place. They paid a small price for intricate carvings in olive wood from the West Bank. Now they were being made to sell abroad. He had heard tourists exclaim how underwhelmed they were with the fourth-century church. They wanted more, expected to be hit by a bolt of lightning or at least by some kind of extreme spiritual awakening. The way he had been the night his father died, when he saw a white dove rise up in front of him and crumble like the dust on the road.

He argued with them about the land, the territory under dispute. His father had fought and his son was fighting now. But he wasn't allowed to ask too many questions. Yusuf had once said, if this is the promised land and promises are broken, then this is a broken land and the only way it can be mended is if a new promise is made.

Saleem filled his palm with sunflower seeds, from a packet he kept in a drawer. He placed one centrally between his teeth, bringing them together until a single crack opened it. With his tongue he manoeuvred the seed, placed it in the side of his cheek, spitting the unwanted outer casing into his other hand. He did this continuously until there were none left. Then he threw the remains in a bin, licked the salt from his lifeline and went off to find his olive oil. A few sunflower seeds were not enough to quell his hunger.

Father George waved at Saleem. Saleem waved back. He

liked the American priest. He had a calming accent, spoke slowly, and occasionally, when they both had time on their hands, which wasn't very often, they played backgammon on a small set Mrs Saleem had given her husband one Christmas. They never played for money, only for prayers. Father George disappeared into the church while Saleem took a moment to pray for those who had passed: his father, their infant child who died at birth, his wife's parents, his neighbour's donkey, much loved and much missed, and all the people he didn't know personally, but who had come, for one reason or another, to bring peace, those from this side of town and those from across the borders.

He remembered years ago, meeting a young girl from England. He had forgotten her name, Maggie or Margaret, but he could still remember her face, round, blue eyes penetrating his, short dark hair, jeans and thick sweater with a snowflake pattern, boots made for tougher weather. She came along with a busload of journalists via Jerusalem, travelled in the cold on Christmas Eve to the capital of Christmas, to listen to the Mayor, a small man with a thick moustache who smiled the whole time he talked, of peace and good will and loving thy neighbour. After he had spoken, he welcomed the group into a spacious room, where men in white robes sat among women in jeans. Tables were piled with food, a banquet like the English girl had never seen before. If he'd had his camera then, Saleem would have taken a picture so he could remember her tears, her delight at being part of such an occasion, her bewilderment at being presented with a sheep's eye on a plate of potato salad.

Christmas celebrations had been cancelled for the past few years, civil ones at least. Saleem missed the music, the festivities, when the whole town gathered and watched dawn break on Christmas Day. Last year a solitary tree stood outside the church, with a few lights, like a sky shot through with only a handful of stars.

After ringing the bell a second time, Saleem left the church, walked to Manger Square, down the steps and on to Beit Sahur Street. It was still early. Tourists were rare, and these days they tended to come and go. Everyone knew Saleem, waved, smiled, croaked out a greeting that only he could comprehend. There was always something waiting for him, cake thick with honey, sweet coffee, fruit which he often accepted and took home to Mrs Saleem.

He took pictures of the street names, of a wooden sign with Bethlehem in bold gold print. He saw a kitten, its desperate meow too painful to hear. He had nothing to offer, except a tickle under the chin, so he walked quickly away and did not look back.

Saleem sat in a coffee shop, windows with cracked panes, radio on the loudest volume. He listened carefully to the news, tut-tutted constantly until the owner told him to stop it. Saleem picked his teeth, shook his head. 'When will it all be over?' he asked Hussein.

Hussein shrugged, 'When it's over,' he said.

When the conflict ended Saleem would ring the bells continuously, so the whole of the world would hear. Every
morning when he woke, he hoped that this was the day. But
it never came.

Saleem drank heavily scented coffee, asked Hussein where
he could buy a photo album for his wife. 'It's a secret,'
Saleem said, pressing one finger tight against his lip. Hussein
threw back his head, then disappeared into the rear of the
shop. He emerged moments later with a dark blue velvet
book, which he offered to Saleem. Saleem took it. His friend
indicated for him to open the book. Saleem opened it. Inside
were photos, some glued down, others floating freely. His
friend said he bought it from the shop that looked like a gro-
cery shop from the outside, but inside you could find
everything if you looked closely enough. 'How much?'
Saleem asked. His friend raised his shoulders, held them
there for a moment, then dropped them.

'Whatever you have,' he said, which meant negotiation, or
in Saleem's case, haggling, which he wasn't very good at,
but which Mrs Saleem was revered for, a talent, he thought,
she was born with, the way others are born with silver
spoons hanging from their mouths.

Saleem finished his coffee, swirled the liquid in the bottom
of the cup and turned it upside down. He chewed on soft
cardamom until the taste had evaporated into his gums, then
turned the cup back over and showed Hussein the marks
left at the bottom. Hussein shook his head. 'See this,' he said,

pointing to something that resembled a divining rod. 'See how it goes and goes . . . and then stops.'

Saleem laughed at Hussein's predictions and walked to Paul VI Street. The stone-walled shop would open soon. He stood outside for a few minutes, knocked on the turquoise door, rattled the shutters pulled down like sleepy eyes. Nothing. He knocked again, harder this time, yelled that he had business to do. Still no response. He read graffiti written in big bold print. *Eternity for all our martyrs.* He raised his eyebrows, held his breath, then released the air slowly.

He slept for an hour then had his lunch of lazy lettuce and juicy tomatoes and the remaining piece of bread, with olive oil and zahtar, and mint tea to wash it down. He walked to the shop again. Low rise houses, dirt tracks, blue sky. How would it feel, he thought, to live in a country with a name that no one is scared to say?

This time the shop was open. He bought two albums for half the asking price. One he would keep for his wife's birthday, the other for their grandchildren, whenever and if ever they came.

He played football outside with some children from the school, before it was time to ring the last bell at half-past two. He said goodbye to Father George and left for home, pleased with his purchases, thinking of where to hide them, away from the searching eyes of Mrs Saleem, who nosed around like it was her part-time job.

Saleem walked along the same road he had walked every

day. From the church to home, on to Manger Square then Milk Grotto Street. He bent down to slip off a shoe because some gravel had found its way in and was rubbing against the sole of his foot.

When he stood up a familiar noise rang out. Five familiar noises. If sounds had colours these were golden. One was too loud and too close. The other four travelled a different road. The rest happened as if in a dream, slowly, no sound, no feeling. There was a flash as his body slumped to the ground. By his side the small, chrome camera, which remained there until they took him away.

The shots came out of the blue and white, green and red and black. From up or down, east or west, Saleem could not tell. Five clear sounds that rang in the calm of afternoon air. Only one hit Saleem, clean and direct. Somewhere inside him a copper-coloured bullet was lodged, its petals blooming into his bone. Any tiny movement and the pain increased fivefold. Someone had been doing their target practice. All Saleem knew was that he was injured, in a part of his body where the blood poured out like a carton of grape juice that had been punctured with a sharp knife. He hadn't realised it was so dark and so red. That he was so dark and so red.

In hospital, Mrs Saleem arrived with noise and fuss and food for her ailing husband. She swayed her head from side to side, until three of her four children came to calm their mother and watched as their father lapsed into unconsciousness. Mrs Saleem saw a white light, as if someone had thrown fairy dust into the air. But instead of settling, it disappeared.

All the bells rang out that day. No one knew who or how or where or why, just that this ordinary man died on an ordinary day in extraordinary circumstances.

Along with Saleem's other belongings, which he kept in an old cigar box at the church, Mrs Saleem was given the camera and the two photo albums. Inside now are pictures of Saleem and his friends, of Hussein and Avraham. Of Mrs Saleem lying asleep, of their children and their house and the street and the church where they held a service for her husband. Of the teapot and Yusuf with his yellowing teeth and their almond tree that bears pink blossom. On the back page is the distorted picture the camera took as it fell. It is of sky and rooftops and white clouds.

(*In reality he lay in the square for four hours until medical help arrived. He was a danger to no one, and had no weapons. He was simply doing his job. He died before medical aid could reach him. Neither side took responsibility. Some say it was the IDF. Others a Palestinian sniper.*)

On the roof of the Church of the Nativity, a thin man with a slightly bent back sits and watches and waits for the sound of continuous bells. He still believes they will come.

Inspired by the true story of Samir Ibrahim Salman, bell ringer at the Church of the Nativity, Bethlehem since 1967. Died April 2002.

Six Geese a-Laying

Sophie Kinsella

We're a fairly exclusive group.

Which OK, I know sounds awful and conceited. If I were talking to anyone else I wouldn't even say it. But *you* understand. This isn't just any antenatal group. You can't just turn up. You have to be chosen.

Petal Harmon, our teacher, conducts all the interviews herself. She isn't affiliated to any of the hospitals or nationwide chains – but let me tell you, she gets enquiries from all over London. People travel miles to be in one of her classes. And she doesn't even advertise. It's all word of mouth.

The women who have had Petal Harmon classes are different. They have a strange look to their eye. They know something the rest of us don't. The thing I've heard said, over and over, is that Petal changed their lives.

Which sounds a *leetle* bit of an exaggeration to me . . . but I take the point. So naturally I applied for her classes as soon as I heard I was pregnant, like everyone else round here. I didn't do anything special at the interview. *So* many girls have asked me if there's some special trick, but all I can say is, I was myself! We talked about my pregnancy . . . and my work in personnel . . . and Dan . . .

Dan's my husband, by the way. He's the one who dropped me off tonight – although he missed the street, and had to go round the one-way system. Which is just typical of him. He said the sign was covered in snow so he couldn't read it . . . but honestly. He's just useless. How he's going to cope with a baby I'll never know!

So where was I? Oh yes. The interview. So I was just very natural, very bubbly, and the next thing I knew, a hand-written card arrived inviting me to the classes.

Obviously I was thrilled. Not that I would gloat or anything. I've barely mentioned it more than a few times to my neighbour Annabel. (She didn't get in, poor love. Even though she took Petal a bunch of flowers and some of those earthy biscuits she makes.) We all feel the same way, all of us in the class. We're not *smug*, obviously not. But the fact that we were all selected gives us . . . I don't know. A little glow. We must have some special quality that the others don't.

There are six of us altogether, all due around the same

time, Christmas. As I walk – well, waddle – into the room, the fire is glowing and the fairy lights are twinkling and it really looks quite Christmassy.

Geraldine's holding forth about something or other, balancing a cup of tea on her bump. She's still in tailored suits, believe it or not. Adjusted to fit, naturally. She had them made up on her last business trip to Singapore.

She's fun, Geraldine . . . but a bit *abrasive*, if you know what I mean. When a midwife came to talk to us Geraldine's first question was 'If you were negligent during my delivery, would I sue you individually or the hospital?'

'So there I am, lying on the couch – and the midwife starts texting her friend!' she's saying now. 'I mean, it's tantamount to negligence, ignoring a patient like that. I'm complaining.'

'Which midwife was it?' asks Georgia alertly. Georgia has blonde highlights, is very posh, and has already put her baby down for Eton and Suzuki violin lessons.

'It was that bloody Davies woman,' replies Geraldine. 'I tell you, I'm writing to the senior midwife, and I'm cc-ing the consultant and my chum in hospital management. I'm going to make her life hell. It's the only way to get results with these people.' She scribbles something in a leather-bound notebook and stuffs it in her Mulberry briefcase.

'I saw my midwife today too,' says Gina, who is sipping her own organic raspberry tea. 'I told her my birth plan. No pain relief.' She smiles contentedly around the room. 'I've told Ralph, as well. I've said to him, even if I beg you. Even if I scream for an epidural!' She leans forward earnestly, her plaits falling over her shoulders. 'Don't listen to me. I won't know what I'm saying.'

Ralph is Gina's partner. He has a goatee beard dyed three shades of red and apparently at the fathers' evening he read out a poem he'd composed himself about placentas. 'You're brave!' says Georgia. 'Didn't Petal say we should be open-minded about pain relief?'

'I've been practising yoga and meditation for years.' Gina looks smug. 'I think I know how to work with my body. It's all in the mind. You can see it as pain . . . or you can see it as empowerment. Plus, Ralph's taken a course in aromatherapy. He's going to make me my own personal blend of oils.'

'He's very *supportive*, Ralph, isn't he?' says Georgia, with a slight frown. Her husband is called Jonno and works non-stop at a merchant bank.

'He's great.' Gina looks smug. 'We really connect, on every level. That's why I'm so confident about labour.'

'And Dan's supportive, isn't he, Ginny?' Georgia turns to me. 'He seems really sweet.'

'Oh, he's crap!' I say with a burst of laughter. 'Utterly useless! He put up the changing table yesterday. I said, if you're as cack-handed as that with the baby I'm not letting you near it—' My laughter's interrupted by the door opening. Petal is there, in her purple crinkly skirt. She really does look like a witch sometimes.

'Are we all here?' she says, her eyes darting around the

room. 'Our special guest speaker has arrived but I'll wait until the whole group is assembled.'

'No Gabby yet,' says Geraldine. 'I know her firm's handling a big merger this week, so . . .' She shrugs. We all know what she means. Gabby hasn't been great at attendance. She always arrives late and often leaves early – and one week she sent along her PA in lieu. It makes you wonder why she's having a baby.

Actually, we know why she's having a baby. It's because her husband wanted one. She's already booked her Caesarean and her 24-hour nanny, and is going back to work three weeks after the birth.

'Last lesson!' says Georgia brightly to Petal. 'If we don't know it now, we never will!'

Petal says nothing for a few moments, just looks at her with that mysterious, slightly eerie gaze she has. 'There are certain lessons each of you has still to learn,' she says at last. Her gaze moves around the room, lingering on each of us in turn. Then she quietly disappears out of the room.

'Oh God,' says Geraldine as the door closes. 'It's the breastfeeding counsellor, I know it. They're worse than Bible-bashers, my friend Lucy said.'

'Breastfeeding raises the IQ,' says Georgia at once. 'Breastfeeding and Mozart. Did you read the article?' She pulls a glossy magazine entitled *Intelligent Baby* out of her bag. 'I'm planning to play the Mozart clarinet concerto every day to my baby.'

There's a sudden flurry of snow against the window, and we all jump in surprise.

'Look at that!' Gina exclaims. 'It's going to be a white Christmas.'

It hasn't snowed like this for years. Real, proper snow. Dickensian snow, Dan called it this morning.

'Speaking of Christmas . . .' Georgia looks around, a little coy. 'Has anyone thought of a name yet?'

'Holly?' says Geraldine with a grin.

'Ivy,' I say with a laugh. 'Or Noel. Dan suggested Bianca. I said, that's the kind of name you *would* think of . . .'

'Only I've thought of one that's rather unusual . . .' Georgia looks around, her mouth twisting with pleasure. 'Melchior.'

'Melchior?' echoes Geraldine. 'You can't call a baby Melchior!'

'I think it's rather lovely,' says Georgia, looking offended. 'For a girl *or* a boy. Mel for short. What do *you* think, Grace?' We all turn to look at Grace in the corner – and as usual, she stares dumbly back with that frightened-rabbit expression she always has.

Now. I'm sure Petal had her reasons for inviting Grace into the class. But frankly . . . she doesn't fit. She's barely out of her teens, for a start. I mean, fancy having a baby at the age of twenty-two! People just don't *do* that any more. So of course she hasn't got the confidence of the rest of us, bless her.

And to be honest, I think it's a shame. The last thing the rest of us need is some drippy, insecure girl bringing us down. Especially when the classes are so oversubscribed. You'd think Petal could have found someone more . . . suitable.

'I haven't even thought about names,' she says, her voice barely above a whisper. 'I just . . .' She swallows. 'I just can't get my head round it.'

'I've got a book you can borrow . . .' begins Georgia.

'Not just that. All of it.' Grace looks imploringly around at the rest of us. 'Motherhood. Being responsible for another life. What if the baby gets ill and I don't recognise the symptoms and it dies? What if I don't bond with it?'

'You'll bond with it,' says Gina in sure tones. 'It's nature.'

'But what if I don't? I listen to you all talking away . . . and I think, how can you all be so confident?' She sounds almost desperate. 'Don't you ever have any worries? Don't you ever doubt yourselves?'

Oh, for goodness sake. This is what I mean. She's all wrong for the class! Maybe some people go to antenatal classes to moan on about their insecurities. But we're just not that kind of women. We know what we want. We know ourselves. Frankly . . . we *don't* have any doubts.

I think it's an age thing.

I glance at Geraldine, who has a perplexed frown. Georgia looks rather blank. Gina is stroking her bump with a beatific smile.

Then Geraldine glances down at her watch.

'I call this a con!' she says. 'We've paid for Petal Harmon's time. Not some jumped-up health visitor—'

The door opens and we all swing round – but it's only Gabby, in her black Formes trousers and jacket, holding her Palm Pilot open and talking into her mobile phone headset.

'Yup,' she's saying. 'Yup. FedEx both of them off. And get me the Anderson figures. OK, I've gotta go now. I'll call as soon as I'm out of this place.' She snaps her Palm Pilot closed and looks around. 'What'd I miss?'

'Nothing,' says Geraldine. 'We've all just been sitting here waiting for some "special speaker". Special rip-off, more like.'

'I assure you.' Petal's calm voice from the back of the room makes us all jump. 'My last speaker is not a rip-off.' She's walking to the front now as Gabby takes her seat. 'I might go so far as to say . . . this last lesson will make the information I have given you in the preceding weeks seem irrelevant.'

There's silence in the room. As Petal looks around there's a faint smile at her lips and her eyes look even more witchy than usual.

'Some of you may have wondered why you were offered places in my class. You will be aware that many women apply but not many are accepted.'

A glow of pleasure creeps over me. As I glance around I can see the same smug smiles on everyone else's faces too. All except Grace, who's looking as petrified as ever.

'Let me just say . . . that I felt you could all benefit particularly from this final lesson.'

She reaches for the switch and dims the light, then draws the door closed. We all exchange glances through the gloom.

'Sounds quite mysterious!' says Geraldine with a laugh. 'I wonder what this is all about.'

'I did once hear a rumour . . .' begins Gina, lowering her voice. 'I heard that Petal Harmon can foresee what kind of labour you're going to have. And that she tells you on your final lesson.'

'I heard she could tell the sex of your baby,' says Gabby, busily texting on her phone. 'But what's the point, with ultrasound? Anyway, I know what kind of labour I'm going to have.'

Suddenly the room goes even darker – although no one's been near the switch. The only light comes from the white glow of the snow outside the window and the tiny luminous buttons of Gabby's mobile.

'Great,' says Georgia, looking up from her notebook. 'How am I going to take notes now? D'you think she'll give out a sheet?'

She stops as the door opens, and we all turn to see a figure standing in the doorway. Tall and slim, wearing a long black dress with a kind of snood affair over her head. Without saying anything she glides into the room and I see she's holding a laptop.

She turns so she's facing us – but still says nothing. The

hood thing is masking her face. All in all, she's hardly the most prepossessing of speakers.

'Not very talkative, is she?' Geraldine whispers in my ear.

The woman dips her hood, reaches for the laptop and switches it on. Visions are flitting across the screen – but whatever CD-Rom she's using, it's not up to much. It's more like some old cine-film. The colours are washed out, and the actions jerky. We all peer silently, our eyes having to adjust.

Then I see it. It's a woman in labour. She's sighing and puffing, her head in her hands.

'Oh for God's sake,' murmurs Geraldine. 'Excuse me?' she says in a louder voice. 'We've seen several videos of giving birth. I really think our last lesson would be better used in discussion, or recapping what we've already covered.'

But the woman doesn't seem to hear her. The images flicker on and we gaze at the screen in silence. It's strangely compelling, even though you can hardly make out what's going on.

'Hang on,' says Georgia suddenly. 'Gina, that's you.'

'*What*?'

We all crane forward and peer at the woman's face.

'Oh my God,' breathes Gina.

'It is!'

'How can it be Gina?'

'I think I've heard about this,' says Geraldine uncertainly. 'Video-empathy. It's to help you visualise your birth. They must have superimposed your head on the screen. It's a bit of a cheap trick.'

'But how have they got Ralph too?' says Gina, sounding freaked out. 'Look!'

Sure enough, on the screen, Ralph is approaching the bed that Gina's lying on. 'Love?' he says. 'I've brought the oils.'

'Ralph . . .' On-screen Gina lifts her head, her face contorted with pain. 'I want pain relief. Proper pain relief.'

'But love, you told me, no pain relief. I'll rub your back with lavender and jasmine . . .'

The sound of Gina's moaning dies away and the screen goes momentarily blank. A moment later she reappears on screen, looking even worse than before.

'Ralph, I need something,' she's panting. 'Please. I've changed my mind.'

'She doesn't,' Ralph is saying to a midwife. 'Look. It's in her birth plan. "Even if I beg, do not give me pain relief. My body will adjust."'

'Please . . .'

'Gina. Love.' Ralph hurries to her side, and strokes her hand soothingly. 'Remember, it's all in the mind. Work *with* your body. That's what you said . . .'

'But I didn't knooow!' Gina's voice rises to a howl. The screen flickers and dies to nothing.

There's a staggered silence. I glance around. Everyone looks stunned.

'Who *are* you, anyway?' Gina's voice bursts out, trembling. 'What right have you got to come in here, making things up . . .'

The woman says nothing, just inclines her head slightly.

My skin starts to prickle all over.

'Maybe she wasn't making it up.' I take a deep breath. 'Are you . . . showing us our futures?'

'Oh, for God's sake,' says Geraldine. 'Get real.'

'I don't believe in mediums,' says Georgia firmly. 'It must be a trick—'

'But how did she do it?' Gina's voice rises in agitation. 'That was me and Ralph! Right there on the screen!'

'I know who it is,' says Grace suddenly. 'It's the Ghost of Babies Future.' She looks at the figure, her face white with fear. 'Is that right?'

There's a taut silence. Then the figure bows her head.

'Oh my God,' says Gina, sounding almost hysterical. 'That was *true*?'

'That's it.' Geraldine's voice snaps. 'I'm not sitting around to hear a lot of ridiculous gobbledegook! I tell you, I'm complaining to Petal Harmon—'

The woman silences her by lifting her hand, and another flickering image appears on the screen.

It's Geraldine. She's sitting on a hospital bed, wincing with pain.

'Just a few details first,' a midwife is saying kindly, pen in hand. 'Then we'll get you sorted out.' She gives Geraldine a sympathetic smile. 'Your name?'

'Geraldine Foster,' puffs Geraldine.

'Ge-ral-dine . . .' the midwife begins writing. Then she stops and her sympathetic smile disappears. 'Geraldine Foster?' she says in a different tone. 'You're the one who complained about me.'

As she moves, the badge on her uniform comes into view. It reads 'Davies'.

'This woman complained to all the big guns!' she's exclaiming indignantly to a second midwife. 'I was given a formal warning. For one lousy text message!'

'She complained about me too,' says the second midwife, and shoots Geraldine a scathing look. 'Said I hadn't followed protocol.'

'Er . . . could I have some pain relief?' Geraldine's voice is strained.

The two midwives look at each other.

'The protocol says we have to examine her thoroughly first,' replies the second. 'I'll fetch some gloves.' She saunters towards the door.

'Will it take long?' Geraldine sounds desperate. Both midwives raise their eyebrows.

'You wouldn't want us to rush things, would you?' says one innocently. 'We'll take as long as we have to.'

The images die away and we all glance awkwardly at Geraldine. She's gone rather pale.

'Listen,' she says at last. 'Ghost. Or whatever you are. Are you showing us things that *will* happen? Or . . . that *might* happen?'

The spirit doesn't reply.

I become aware that Gabby is murmuring into her mobile phone. I don't think she's even noticed what's been going on.

'Look, I'm sorry,' she says, getting up from her chair. 'Crisis at work. I've got to go. Thanks very much for the presentation, but to be brutally honest, this baby stuff doesn't really interest me . . .'

She breaks off, as a kind of angry flash comes from the spirit. On the screen appears an image of Gabby in a maroon suit, holding a baby. She's just standing there in a white room, holding a tiny baby, while in the background someone's shouting 'Gabby! Taxi's here!'

Her face is utterly stricken.

'Gabby!' comes the voice again. 'You'll be late! Just bring the baby down, he'll be fine with the nanny—'

A tear trickles down the on-screen Gabby's face. Then another. Then another.

I risk a glance at Gabby. She's staring at the screen, transfixed. There's a faint sheen to her eyes.

'Er . . . Tristan . . .' she says into her mobile. 'I'll be along later. Yes well, *this* is important.' She snaps her phone shut and quietly takes her seat again.

There's a subdued atmosphere, and I can't help feeling a rising apprehension.

'I can't believe it's all doom and gloom!' says Georgia defiantly. 'I'm sure some of us are going to have perfectly wonderful labours and gorgeous babies!' She looks around as though for support. 'And I'm certainly not going back to work. I'm going to devote myself to my child!'

The spirit seems to regard her thoughtfully for a moment. The next moment, an image of Georgia appears on a screen. She's breastfeeding a baby in a vast, expensive kitchen, while Mozart plays in the background.

'There,' says Georgia smugly. 'I knew it! Of course, I have prepared for this baby *very* thoroughly . . .'

The image fades away and is replaced by one of a small boy in a school playground.

'Milky . . . Milky . . .' a gang of boys is chanting around him.

'Don't call me Milky!' he yells desperately. 'I'm Mike!'

'No you're not! You're Milky Melchior!'

The images fade away and Georgia clears her throat.

'All children are teased,' she says, sounding a little discomfited. 'It's perfectly normal.'

Another image comes into view. This time a man in his twenties is at the entrance to a smart restaurant together with a blonde girl, her hair in a very peculiar hairstyle. The place looks rather like the Savoy Grill, although they've done a few strange things to it . . .

'My name's . . . Mel.' His face twitches in a nervous tic.

'Are you all right?' says the *maître d*'.

'I'm fine.' He gives a tight smile and hands over his coat. Then, as piped music becomes audible through the loud-speakers, his whole body seems to tense. 'Oh my God. No.'

'The music,' says the blonde girl urgently to the *maître d'*. 'Can you turn off the music?'

'I can't stand it.' The young man's hands are to his head and he's heading for the door. 'I can't stand it!'

'It's the Mozart clarinet concerto!' the blonde girl shoots over her shoulder as she hurries after him. 'He's phobic!'

The images die away. I dart a glance at Georgia – and she looks utterly shellshocked.

'I knew it.' Grace's trembling voice comes from the back. 'That's why we were picked for this class. Because things were going to go wrong for us.'

The spirit lifts her head and seems to look directly at Grace. And all of a sudden a new image is on the screen.

It's Grace. Her figure has snapped back into shape, she's had a new haircut and is walking jauntily down the street. In fact, if I'm utterly, grudgingly honest . . . she looks better than anyone.

Must be her age.

Now she's sitting in a café, holding her baby and sipping a smoothie. The baby starts to cry, and with expert ease she slips a finger into its mouth and carries on drinking. She looks totally content and natural.

'Your hair's fab!' says Georgia. 'Where do you go?'

'I dunno,' says Grace in bewilderment. 'I never cut my hair.' She peers at the screen. 'I don't understand. What's wrong? What's the catch?'

'Nothing, apparently,' says Gina, sounding a little petulant.

'Maybe that's what you had to learn, Grace,' says Geraldine, sounding kinder than I've ever heard her. 'That it would all be OK.'

I'd murmur some agreement – except that I'm feeling too tense to speak. I'm the only one in the room who hasn't seen her future yet.

'So . . . what about me?' I try to give a casual laugh. 'What's going to happen to me?'

There's a pause. Then the spirit nods, and the screen lights up again.

Even though I was expecting it, I can't help feeling a jolt as I see myself on the screen. I'm holding a baby, watching Dan as he taps at a crib with a hammer.

'You're useless!' I'm saying. 'It's a *rocking* crib. It should bloody rock!'

The image segues straight into another one. Dan's changing the baby's nappy while I hover behind.

'That's not how the tabs go!' I'm snapping. 'You've done it wrong!'

As I hear my own voice I feel an uncomfortable twinge. I never realised before how sharp it was.

And I've never seen Dan with that hurt expression before.

I stare, transfixed, as my screen-self turns towards him – and he quickly wipes it away with a smile.

'Well you're OK too, Ginny,' says Georgia, sounding a little piqued. 'Everything's fine!'

'It's not.' My voice sounds a little hoarse to my own ears.

Now the images are coming thick and fast. Dan with me and the baby at home. At the shops. At the park. And a constant soundtrack of my own voice, snapping at him. 'You're useless!' 'That's wrong!' 'Give it here, I'll do it!'

Shut up! I want to yell at myself. Leave the poor man alone!

But my screen-self just keeps on relentlessly, hectoring and criticising. And all I can see is Dan's face, gradually closing in on itself. Until he looks as though he doesn't want to know any more. As though he's had enough.

I feel a shaft of panic.

'Spirit . . .' I say quickly. 'You didn't answer the question before. Are these the things that *will* happen? Or that *might* happen?'

I look up. But the room is empty. The spirit's gone.

Slowly the lights are coming up.

I look around – and the others are all blinking. Georgia's rubbing her eyes. Gabby looks as if she's in a trance.

As though from nowhere, Petal has materialised at the front of the room.

'That was your final lesson,' she says in soft tones. 'I'll ask you all now a small favour. I would prefer that the exact contents of my classes be kept to yourselves.'

We all give stupefied nods. I don't think any of us can quite speak.

'Please, take a few moments to gather yourselves.' Petal smiles around at us. 'You can leave whenever you're ready. And . . . good luck. All of you.'

Before any of us can say anything, she makes her way to the doorway and vanishes. We sit in dazed silence for a few moments. Then there's a small crash as *Intelligent Baby* slithers off Georgia's lap on to the floor.

'Here you are,' says Gina, picking it up. Georgia surveys it for a few moments.

'Thanks,' she replies. She takes it from Gina's hand and rips the whole thing in two.

There's a scuffling next to me, and I see Geraldine pulling her leather notebook out of her bag. She rips out the page on which she'd written 'Davies – COMPLAIN' and crumples it up. 'There,' she says, and exhales sharply.

'Does anyone want to go for a drink?' says Gabby suddenly. 'I could do with one.'

'Absolutely,' says Georgia in heartfelt tones.

'Me too,' says Grace, stepping forward. Her cheeks are glowing and she looks like a new woman. She shakes her hair back, as though practising for her new style. 'I'm in no hurry.'

'Sod the baby,' says Gina. 'I need a double vodka.'

'Ginny?' Geraldine looks at me. 'You coming?'

'You all go,' I say. 'I . . . have to get home. Now.'

When I arrive home, Dan's in the nursery. He looks up as I approach, and for the first time ever I notice the wary look in his eyes.

'I'm trying to make up this crib,' he says. 'But it won't rock.' He shoves it in frustration. 'I don't know what the hell's wrong with it—'

'It doesn't matter.' I cut him off. 'None of it matters. Come here.' I hold out my arms and Dan looks at me in startled bemusement.

I feel a small icy plunge.

It's too late. It's all too late.

Then, slowly, Dan puts down his screwdriver. He comes forward and takes me in his arms, and I find myself clinging on to him.

'Happy Christmas,' I say, my voice muffled with emotion. 'And . . . and thank you. For making the crib. And everything. Thank you for everything.'

'That's OK!' says Dan with a surprised laugh. 'Happy Christmas to you too, darling.' He smiles down at me, stroking my bump. 'And Happy Christmas to this little one.'

For a while we're silent, the two of us, standing by the window arm in arm as the snow falls endlessly outside.

The three of us, I should say.

God Bless Us Every One keeps running through my head, over and over.

But naturally I don't voice it aloud.

Instead, after a while I murmur, 'You know, I was thinking about names.'

'Really?' Dan looks up. 'Any ideas?'

'Well . . . I was thinking we probably *shouldn't* call it Melchior . . .'

Seven Swans a-Swimming

Helen Cross

In the natural world, the concept of faithfulness in sexual partners remains largely the province of birds rather than mammals, and even some of the most monogamous birds have been known to stray from their mates.

World Wildlife Fund, August 2001

It was 8.15 p.m. on New Year's Eve and my handsome neighbour was lying naked in the frost. Immediately I knew I'd found another victim – not of a seasonal serial killer, but of the lovestruck madness that had infected my little community.

He had all the symptoms – he was breathing quickly as if lusty and spellbound, his fists were clenched, his cheeks flushed. And when he rose up, bewitched, maddened, it was as if he'd sipped on a potion because as he stood there the moon was nothing more than his spotlight, the grass his soft green stage. He was not snoring, or smashed – just wide eyed and watching the smoky sky.

Of course one of the symptoms of my sudden erotic lunacy that year was a strange tendency towards the fabulous – and that New Year's night I didn't see a *handsome man*, I saw a *sex god*. When I moved further along the fence and looked more closely it was nothing so amazing: the unnamed neighbour, the fireman, was not a god and not quite naked – he wore boxer shorts. But definitely, I could tell he was afflicted, just as the violinist was, and the headmistress, Bride, Lola the weather girl, the anaesthetist. And, maybe more than anyone, me myself.

I inhaled sharply and heard an icy shattering: the splintering of all my marital promises. The fireman moaned and I wanted to cry out from where I was crouched, for it was a moan that shot a deep ache right through me.

One year earlier.

'A waterway,' Nick, my husband, exclaimed, 'as in Venice!'

'Canal,' I replied, looking over his shoulder at the architect's scribbly modern house, 'as in corpse-filled relic of an industrial wasteland.'

'Swans, boats and bulrushes . . .' Nick continued.

'I'm not sure I like swans.'

Nick looked at me sadly. We were not getting along well. We had been together for seven years, but married for just one. We had a four-month-old baby, Billy. Our problems could be boiled down to something typical: he had become preoccupied with his busy job, me with my new son. Our sex life had suffered. We were constantly tired and irritable. We found battlegrounds everywhere; that day it was where we would live.

Though our flat was obviously too small I was reluctant to move. Nick had his hopes set on something city centre and executive. I tried to tell him that the whole Water's Edge development was too conventional for us. Just because we're married didn't mean we had to change, I argued. 'Let's give it all up, Nick, traipse around fields in a caravan eating nettles.'

'But I like the combination of the city and nature. I want wildlife in my wild life.'

'There's nothing wild about it,' I exclaimed. 'It reminds me of horrible petty repressed places, like Stratford-upon-Avon.'

'Stop being so contrary,' Nick replied sharply. 'We're thirty-three, we're married, we've got Billy, we have to grow up. I like swans.'

'You know that nowadays property tycoons design them,' I said petulantly. 'They're battery powered.'

*

Around this time I confessed to Nick the other thing that unnerved me about Water's Edge. I'd read in the paper that it was where the woman who had been chosen as Bride 2004 was to live.

Bride was blonde and twenty-five. She was a fit account-ant, an adored only child, a once upon a time ballet dancer, gymnast and stage-school star. Thanks to a competition on a local radio station, Bride was to be married, to a complete stranger she had yet to meet.

I knew it was tacky, sensational and symptomatic of our celebrity-saturated culture, but Bride's story fascinated me.

'*I've seen friends leave it too late,*' Bride confessed huskily in her first interview. '*I want to commit and now.*' To win the competition Bride had to answer ten general knowledge questions, such as '*Three mammals that mate for life are the wolf, the dik-dik and the beaver.*' She also had to cheerily answer suggestive phone-in questions from the public. '*It's oh oh oh oh – no "a" – the spelling is m-o-n-o-g-o-m-o-u-s*' was the only question she answered incorrectly. Then she had to choose a favourite bird: '*Hey, I'm an old romantic: the swan*'. Finally Bride had to submit a photograph, which was judged by the readers of the evening paper. She won by a mile. Her prize included not only a symmetrical man (twenty-six, blond, tanned, muscular, called Mark, a mar-keting executive), but also a Range Rover, a year's worth of manicures, pedicures and hairstyling, and a 'luxury pad' on Water's Edge.

'Lucky woman,' Nick said when I finished telling Bride's story. Then, as he turned away from Billy and me to fall asleep, he said, 'Now watch her mess it up.'

Six months later, Lola landed in my marriage.

'They love each other,' I said to Lola as we watched the eight swans float before the foundations of our new house. In my lap Billy thrashed like a fat fish. The birds were so mesmerisingly calm that I had to admit their beauty even if they were assembled in builders' warehouses as estate dressing.

'Maybe they just don't have the bottle to split up,' Lola said.

She said breezily, I thought, because Lola was a weathergirl. She was the pretty, new, single, Spanish mate of my husband Nick. They worked together at the TV station. In just three months Lola had pushed up through the cracks in my marriage like a bright weed. Nick said he'd struck up a friendship with her because she was also, shrewdly, buying property on Water's Edge. Apparently, the pair discussed house prices in the canteen. Lola's apartment was described as 'top end' and had one bedroom, a Jacuzzi, sauna and panoramic city views.

'Counselling,' I shouted to Lola, as Billy thrashed and kicked and howled. 'Perhaps they've worked it through and have decided to make a go of it. For the sake of the cygnets.'

'Even cygnets know when there's an atmosphere,' Lola *snapped icily*, blowing smoke over the water and sighing. Weed, I thought.

Yes, if I'd been a proper wife Lola would've been dealt with – poisoned, pulled up by the roots, cut down with a spade – but I was faint with sleeplessness, and I'd been faithful to Nick for seven years and was exhausted by our constant bickering, and in turn rather fascinated by that Spanish woman who lit her cigarettes dramatically, as if she was famous.

Bride was married that June. It was a summer of racial unrest, of fights on the streets, fear and anger, dark talk of strangers in our midst, but Bride knocked it all off the top spot. She was the headlines. On the big day the evening paper produced a glossy Wedding Special. Everything appeared effortless. I read Nick excerpts from the speeches given at the reception. '*Mating for life is now rare*,' Best Woman declared. '*Animals who practise monogamy make up only a handful of species, but I know this girl, and she's no ordinary mammal. She's determined to make this work.*'

In the next four months Billy learned to walk, and above our dizzyingly expensive canal-side homes came SuperGym Inc., to the right Aqualife Experience, and to the left 'Europe's smartest car park'. 'Well our souls may wither and die, Nick, but we'll have somewhere safe to leave the car,' Lola *quips drily*, when we meet up at lunchtime to look at the development.

Gazing at the swans and the high gates it occurred to me that Nick and I had done something dangerous and wrong – built a romantic union, and now a home, based entirely on keeping other people out.

While preparing to leave our tiny attic flat Nick and I junked all our second-hand furniture. I took my student clothes to the charity shop. I ditched Nick's cricket whites, football programmes and walkie-talkies. My collection of chipped pre-war crockery we smashed in celebration of our new, sensible married lives.

Throwing stuff out always made me queasy. Around now I began to wonder if, like the city's murderous rioters, change was the thing I most feared. And if this was the reason I'd married Nick in the first place.

Lola took a day off work to help us move, and with Nick she carried the student futon out to the skip. We'd bought an expensive new divan. Lola patted the lumpy old mattress and said, 'Bet this has seen some action, tiger,' and Nick looked at her shyly, and for a moment I was excited, for it was like seeing a photograph of someone I used to know.

'Have you heard of Bride?' I asked Lola later that day.

'Heard of her? Hell, I could have *been* her! I applied. But they didn't think I looked like the faithful type,' Lola *giggled brightly*.

Unsettled, Nick and I settled in. Billy began, fearlessly, to climb, jump and run. The eight swans, jewelled in their loyal bliss by raindrops, which trembled like a shower of diamonds on snow, watched us all steadily. All day they patrolled the stretch of black water, gazing their pitch-black stares into our living room as we young homemakers unpacked our boxes. I tried not to glare back at those perfectly serene and stable pairs, who seemed to mock my increasingly brittle and unsteady marriage.

'Hey, yours is sooooo traditional,' Lola *said sunnily* when she came round for drinks. 'Mine's more like the pad of a high-class hooker.'

Still, having that minx around was strangely invigorating. Just seeing Lola reminded me of uncomfortable but vitalising adult questions, like, is it possible for a man to love two women at once? Do singles have better sex lives? Can, with stretching longevity, humans realistically be faithful for life?

'You know what, Lola, I realise now that this house is rather like the place Nick grew up in,' I said.

'That's why I like it,' Nick replied.

I was shot with a memory: of the disappointment I felt when I realised all the women Nick had ever dated looked the same – like trusted comfortable shoes bought over and over by a man who hated shopping.

'But, Nick, you're gonna feel like you've married your mother,' Lola *said warmly*. And Nick gave her a look of confusion as if to say, *of course* – he'd always intended to marry his mother.

Around this time I bought the paper daily for updates on Bride's marriage. On 24 November Bride's builder father was interviewed about rumours of matrimonial trouble. *'She's not single any more. She's married,'* he stated solemnly, *'and now the girl has to learn to want what she's got, not get what she wants.'*

One Saturday in early December we left Billy with his grandmother for the first time, and invited our new neighbours round for housewarming drinks. 'Husband,' Nick said, stretching out his hand to the banker, 'as in man of the house.'

'Wife,' I replied, 'as in dangerously bored wild cannon.'

Madly, I'd sent a handwritten invitation to the radio station for Bride, but the celebrity wife did not appear. The nearest thing we had to a star was Lola, wearing a tiny fairy outfit in sheer gauze. The fireman from across the water came to the party, and stood smouldering at the edges of rooms. Intoxicated, I wandered over to him with more wine. His chest was full as if he was perpetually inhaling and I wondered if this indicated repression, shyness or fitness. His hips were slim and firm. Mister, you and me could slip into sex as easily as filling this glass, I thought drunkenly.

But whenever I turned my head I could hear my married, monogamous guests talking about inflation, crime, careers, circular saws and other riveting topics. Even by midnight ours remained a danceless, kissless party. 'Come and meet Donald,' Nick shouted.

'Sorry, can't stop,' I waved, 'I have to go and put my head in the oven.'

'BRIDE IN MARRIAGE CRISIS', it said one startling day in mid-December, beside a picture of her, blurred, hurrying away towards a Range Rover, dark in sunglasses, dry-cleaning folded over one arm, a pink bouquet in the other. Bride looked scared and tearful. She made the choice seem stark: live married and be frustrated, but with comfort, security and riches, or stride for liberation, freedom and self-expression – and get a lifetime's supply of panic and anxiety as your introductory gift.

Deep winter came, icy and chill, but my executive home was so comfortable, warm and familiar that I felt constantly dozy. Sedated so thoroughly by monogamy I found it hard to get out of the chair. Nick was working late every night. My nagging, his raving, our constant preoccupation with how things used to be, was getting worse.

When Billy slept for one single hour each afternoon I tried to cheer up by sitting on the frozen strip of gravel outside the front door. I was often to be seen cuddling my cup of coffee, throwing expensive pâtisserie to the trusty swans.

Some days, *en route* from her hooker's pad to the TV station, the breezy weathergirl came to visit me. I was the lunatic client and Lola my efficient caseworker. 'What the hell is it with you and those goddamned swans,' she *said frostily*, one day. She was waving her arms around in comic imitation of a Mafia boss. 'Is there something going on here that I should know about, honey?'

'Oh Lola,' I confessed. 'Perhaps I'm jealous. They're the only happy couples I know.'

On 20 December, in response to much rumour and speculation, Bride gave an interview. She insisted that for the last six months she'd been a good wife. Then cheekily let slip that she sometimes wondered how good she would be at being a bad wife.

I panicked when I read this. Was Bride really going to throw up the glitter, attention and acclaim and put a torch to her marriage? I felt dizzy. I decided to talk things over with Nick. We had to improve our relationship before it was too late.

Then Nick came in exhausted from work and said, 'He thinks they're going to roast our swans next.'

'Who thinks?'

'The guy two doors down. Hungry foreign crooks are gonna cook our native birds! For Christmas dinner.'

For months now there had been unrest, protests, demands for all foreigners to be sent home. Regularly our local news reported blood-soaked scenes where fearful men fought one another.

'You know what, Nick,' I said sadly. 'Since we got married you and I've become afraid of all we don't know.'

'I'm just protecting my family.'

'You've not been having enough sex.'

'How do you know?'

That evening rumours about the city's asylum seekers roasting the swans knocked Bride out of the headlines. The editor wrote in the paper that the birds would not be cooked on a blue sparked wood fire by true hunters, but crammed into a council oven and baked '*at the taxpayer's expense*'. ('*Immigrants are regularly scoffing the Queen's birds!*')

Energised, I imagined a huge, stiff-necked swan stuffed

and gently roasting, waxy juices spooling like milk into the olive river water.

In the days before Christmas Nick went to office parties and I stayed at home with the door locked, watching the Christmas tree. I twiddled with my wedding ring and tried not to think about Bride. I stopped getting the paper. Then, accidentally, I heard on the radio that Bride had visited a doctor. And that she'd confessed to her friend that she was trying her best to stick it out but she'd seen pigs with better table manners, and she didn't get where she is today by following a man around picking up his socks.

Then, when I couldn't bear the torpor, and the tension between Nick and me any longer, everything changed. It was the afternoon of Christmas Eve. The transformation came as dramatically as the weather shifting suddenly from rain to shine. But, as I later would tell my fireman neighbour, I heard nothing – no gunshot, flapping or the elastical snapping of a stretched neck. He heard nothing either, no final insult, no breaking of a last straw – but it had happened: the ornithological symbol of monogamous happiness had flown the nest.

Only later did I link the disappearance of the bird with my own sudden shift in mood. Even before I noticed that there were only seven swans I'd flung my head back and looked up at the leaden sky and cried out, a deep and distinctly female moan.

Three angry local residents found no carcass or feathers, despite a fingertip search. The police were informed but by evening still there were just seven white bells catching a cold moonlight.

That night I was sure I detected the seven moving more quickly – alert and agitated by their new number, energised by the newly single one.

In a leader, the editor ignored the growing social unrest and wrote, '*It's impossible to predict what Bride will do next.*'

'They were infatuated with one another,' I said to my fireman neighbour when he appeared at my side on the towpath as if by magic. It was just after midnight, only a few minutes into Christmas Day. Billy, who was sleeping deeply through the night now, was curled in his cot. Nick was still out dancing. I felt chilly, I trembled inside, as if the door to my heart was flung wide open – a Welcome mat hovering on the step. Wildly, I wondered if the man would swing me over his shoulder and carry me off to his lair.

'That's not infatuation,' the fireman replied gently, pointing at the frosty birds. 'It's just survival; one has to stay in the nest keeping the eggs warm, while the other goes out to get food.'

'You mean it's nothing more than incubation?' I exclaimed, pressing a fingertip to my lips. 'They were only staying together for the children?' An electric surge of flirtation shook me. 'Now, that can't be right, can it?'

When I'd cleared up all the wrapping paper and Nick was settled with his gadgets and Billy had broken most of his toys, I turned on the radio for news. '*I'm young*,' an amused voice cried. '*I need fun; it was all a terrible mistake.*'

I locked the door. I must settle down with my family. Be calm. Loyal and faithful. Achieve monogamous, domestic bliss. The challenge I faced was to appear sexually lewd, adventurous and flirtatious, to keep Nick interested; while also being clean, watchful, organised and busy, to keep my baby safe. Surely, with a bit of determination it could be done.

Then just before midnight, accidentally I glanced out at the still seven swans and saw the fireman's pretty wife leaving with a child in each hand, and a rucksack slung over her shoulder.

The next morning, Boxing Day, men and women spilt out of their waterside houses to see our celebrity: the lonely swan. Children curled their new bikes along the towpath. There were snowball fights between the sexes. A sledge appeared and couples pulled one another, laughing.

'Look at her – she's so confused,' the headmistress said. 'Heartbroken.'

'No wonder! The others hate her now,' the anaesthetist said. 'A singleton's always a threat to couples.'

'How do you know it's a she?' the illustrator asked, arriving with a bunch of mistletoe.

'Perhaps he had trouble with commitment. He thought he wanted to mate for life, but in the end he realised, no,' Nick suggested.

'That's understandable,' I agreed, smiling at Nick excitedly.

With giggles and mock embarrassment we residents gave one another little puckered kisses under the mistletoe. And after lunch we gathered again. We couldn't settle. We made snowmen and snowwomen with carrot noses and raisin smiles – lips that soon melted into wide, wet, gagging mouths.

On Boxing Day evening Bride was discovered at her father's house where she was soon besieged by the press. She was filmed wearing a black diaphanous dressing-gown on the doorstep. Journalists hurled questions. They wanted to know what she would do next. Bride smiled. She dipped her head, raised her dazzling blue eyes and stared straight into the camera. She pouted and soaked up the flashlights. Sultrily, slowly, she said, 'I plan to slip into something a little less comfortable – and then go out for a drink.'

The next day, 27 December, all the residents were outdoors again, drinking straight from the bottle. Billy jumped, shouted and rolled in the snow. Nick and I tried to guess which swan was single, and which was still in a couple. Which wings were folded indignantly, which were loose with possibility. Which swan looked like an exhausted nag, which like a joyful free spirit.

The headmistress brought out rum punch, the violinist a chocolate log. Leftover crackers were cracked and party hats worn. Confidently I watched the fireman and he watched me. Was he thinking what I was thinking: that the seven swans were the best Christmas present we'd ever had?

That night the temperature dropped sharply.

Nick was agitated. Lola had gone to her mother's for Christmas, but on 28 December she called to say she was mad with boredom and was coming back to throw a party in her apartment.

It began to snow harder and deeper.

The following evening, as fifty guests pressed into Lola's tiny luxury kitchen in hot festive spirit, I returned Billy to his grandmother's house. Later I saw the anaesthetist kissing the professor of mathematics. The computer analyst joining the PR man in the Jacuzzi. You couldn't see the panoramic city views because the windows were so steamed with hot breath. After midnight the drunken anaesthetist and the violinist ran down the six flights of stairs and through the blizzard's white whirl and dived into the icy canal, sinking for an alarming moment under the water. The party followed, to watch the couple rise with coughs, laughter and sneezes.

Seven stern beaks hung open an inch. Then there was a shout and Lola, shrieking, leapt into the water. There was applause as she spluttered and splashed, raised her fist in freezing triumph. Sodden, Lola danced around to warm herself on the towpath and was cuddled for warmth by Nick, and then she jumped in again, and again, and more bodies, including the bald illustrator, the headmistress and a skinny dog, followed Lola, shouting passionately.

That night the paper printed '*Bride's Ten Tips for the Best New Year Ever*'. These included, at number six, 'Kiss strangers', number three, 'Wear little', and at number one, 'Regret nothing'.

On New Year's Eve I came in from a walk with my son to discover my phone flashing a message: 'Don't wait up, darling. I have to work late. I'll be back in the morning.' Then minutes later there was another, this time from Lola: 'Hell, I'm as surprised as you are. I didn't intend this to happen, no way. It's weird but we can't help ourselves.'

Without saying a word, or feeling anything other than a huge excitement, I took Billy to his grandmother's again, and went upstairs to change.

Because I felt unseasonably hot, it was no hardship to crunch through the snow in that tiny sparkling outfit. I crossed the bridge at a steady trot, and soon I saw my fireman, lying on the grass in his garden. Crouched, sick with possibility and aching, I imagined the astonished thrill of a bird the first time it ran, soared and flew.

Far away I think I saw the headmistress coming home with a stranger, the violinist leaving with a magnum of champagne, and a pretty woman, who I imagined to be the flitting Bride, striding in a white trouser suit, her gait that of one with a feather balanced on the tip of her nose.

'Kiss me, you,' I hissed through the fence. 'Whoever you are, kiss me.'

It was all I could say because I didn't even know his name – we were strangers in a big city – but it worked and the man, as he prowled the garden, heard and came sniffing towards my hiss like a horny dog. Before he saw me he sensed me, steadily he looked at me, then unlatched his gate.

Through the darkness and the snow he came, to where his hissing, flushed, half-dressed married neighbour crouched in the New Year snow.

Such love surely happens every night in every city in the land, but that moonlit meeting between me and an unknown man felt unique and romantic. It took me from one year into the next and lived on in my dreams until I was a very old woman.

As I said to my husband the next day, perhaps every now and then you have to unbridle your lust and face what you fear. Nick disagreed, he said he'd learned that love really is what you do with what you've got. I'm still not sure, but in the weeks that followed, when I watched Lola looking at me sheepishly through her curls, or saw Bride laughing at us on TV, I understood what perhaps every beautiful bird knows – sometimes in life you will taste one way of loving, and sometimes the other.

Eight Maids a-Milking

Ben Richards

It's when Hans tells me the name of his daughter's Christmas show that I suddenly remember Scott and Eva.

It can happen like that sometimes; a Friends Reunited in your head, people you thought were lost and gone for ever suddenly flash into your consciousness (or sneak into your subconscious if it's under cover of a dream). It's often girls: especially the ones you regret not sleeping with, but also old girlfriends and their sisters. Sometimes it's those you've fallen out with or no longer see, and sometimes it's just weird people you have no business remembering.

Mostly they're uninvited.

My life has been a long and boring battle with alcohol and – to a lesser extent – drugs. On the whole I took drugs to be able to drink more, so alcohol was always the primary problem. But as a result of their combination, I've sat in a lot of living rooms and had very intense times with very many people over a number of years. I was going to say intense, meaningless times but I'm not quite sure if that's true. Some are one-offs – the babbling lunatics who start to talk backwards, some you get to know pretty well (as you would expect, having had exactly the same conversation with them over the course of a few years). And then you either die or you straighten yourself out – as I hope I have – but either way those people are gone, you'll never see them again unless it's by chance; their numbers are deleted from your mobile because even if you could see them again, they spell big trouble.

Sometimes you think about them, though.

Scott and Eva.

The particular living room in which I'm sitting belongs to a German called Hans. I don't know him that well but he's a friend of a friend and I've done some carpentry for him. He lives in one of the Docklands flats that has its own little quayside where kids canoe in summer. Hans doesn't spell trouble at all, big or small. If he spelled trouble I would have known him as German Hans like all the troublesome French Saras, American Petes and Scottish Gerrys I have known. Put their nationality in front of their name and it means they're barflies and caners. But Hans isn't German Hans, he makes worthy film documentaries and he's hiding from trouble behind his Christmas tree, peering out of the window for the gang of kids from the local estate that has been terrorising his family for the last six months.

Hans's problems started when he told some kids off for vandalising a bike that wasn't even his. Rule number one: don't engage with leery kids, they will just make your life a misery. Rule number two: don't remonstrate with them if you have a German accent. Especially on the Isle of Dogs. Poor Hans – a harmless beardy, a documentary film maker – has since suffered the agony of having them ring constantly on the doorbell, follow him when he leaves the house, bait and taunt his family for being asylum seekers, throw stones at the window, threaten his wife and daughter (who is six) with various brutal sexual assaults.

My best and oldest friend, Patrick – who used to spell trouble but doesn't any longer – shrugged when I told him about the persecution of Hans and said it was class war on the Isle of Dogs; the revenge of the have-nots against the moneyed interlopers. Patrick has been 'dying' of hepatitis C since pretty much for ever. I used to go round to keep him company in his illness and we would indulge in our favourite pastime of writing letters of complaint to bank managers, TV companies and tube bosses. Now I realise he will outlive everybody but I still go round there so we can continue our birds-with-wounded-wings-battered-by-the-great-storm-of-life routine. We've found a new game now, which is gatecrashing internet discussion forums in order to start cyber-wars between the participants. You have to find one that doesn't have threads because, apart from being difficult to follow, you can easily become marginalised.

I tried to explain to Patrick that I felt sorry for Hans, whose only crimes were to be German and make films about disappearing tribes in the Amazon. Hans felt a sense of civic duty when he saw a gang of kids vandalising somebody else's bike and now he is paying a price which is both ridiculous and humiliating. 'What does he think you can do about it?' Patrick asked. It was a question that I had asked myself, coming to the conclusion that Hans thought that because I worked with my hands as a carpenter I was hard enough to see off his tormentors. Patrick sneered and said that Hans was probably going through bad karma for the Blitz and I shouldn't interfere. There's an old song by the Specials called 'What I like most about you is your girlfriend'. It's a good example of a title being far better than the song itself but it's true in Patrick's case and I'm only sorry they never did a follow-up called 'Why your girlfriend hasn't left you yet is a mystery up there with the origins of life on earth'.

Anyhow, I did feel sorry for Hans, whether his relatives flew a Junkers 88 over the Isle of Dogs half a century ago or not. And I felt sorry for his nice wife Gudrun who was tormented by this persecution and their little kid Katty who had to hold her dad's hand as he tried not to walk too fast or show his fear in front of a crowd of teenagers mocking his accent and telling him to fuck off back to Kosovo. Tonight, because Katty was appearing in her school's Christmas show, her dad had swallowed his pride and asked me to walk with them from the house to the school because it was cold and dark and he was scared of a gang of teenage kids and the damage they might do to his daughter.

And so I said yes, although this was just moral support because anybody can give a slap to a couple of thirteen-year-old kids; it's when their crim dad turns up and wants to cap you for it that you've got to worry. I love expressions like that: cap you, clip you, whack you. It makes it sound like a good thing, something cool and clean and vaguely chic. Not like having a lump of metal smash violently into your head and spill those flickering memories of babbling drug fiends and girlfriends' sisters all over the gutter. I often wonder what it would be like, whether it would hurt.

But Hans is desperate because he wants to get Katty safely to her show and he needs somebody to come with him and I agree and so now we're sitting drinking whisky (Hans) and peppermint tea (me) and I ask him what the show is and he tells me that they're doing a stage version of the Twelve Days of Christmas. And I start singing it backwards although I always get the Drummers and the Pipers mixed up, waiting to get to Five Gold Rings because that's the best bit of course (Five Go-old Rings!) but when I get to Eight Maids a-Milking I stop.

Eight Maids a-Milking.

Scott and Eva.

I also stop singing because little Katty has just walked into the room dressed as some kind of bird, although for the life of me I can't tell whether she is Turtle-Dove, French Hen or Partridge.

'Look at you!' I say and she twirls around.

'What am I?' she asks, which catches me out for a second but luckily I see that she has a piece of string around her neck, hanging from which are some cardboard cut-out pears.

'You're only the Partridge,' I say. 'How did you get the starring role in the show?'

She stares at me suddenly.

'Will the boys shout at us tonight?'

I clench my fists in anger. She's the Partridge in the Pear Tree for fuck's sake, she shouldn't be worrying about stuff like that.

'Nah,' I say. 'Anybody shouts at us tonight and me and your dad'll chase them down the street and throw them in the river.'

'And drown them?' she asks.

'Most definitely. We'll do that after we've tortured and shot them.'

Hans frowns. Torturing somebody is no laughing matter and cracking jokes about it with kids is obviously strictly *verboten*. I return his dirty look. If he wasn't such a liberal he wouldn't be in this mess because: (a) he wouldn't have given a toss about them smashing up his neighbour's bike and (b) he wouldn't need me around.

Katty sings, 'Torture, shoot and drown them.'

'It's the only language they understand,' I say and Hans scowls and looks like he's going to say something. Instead, he goes off to the bathroom to have a shave and I walk over to the window and look out at the light from the buildings shifting and stirring just beneath his balcony.

There's a song by Steve Earle which is probably one of my favourite ever songs where he says that he can't remember if he said goodbye.

I don't think I ever said goodbye to Scott and Eva.

Scott played the bass and had been in a number of bands. He seemed to have pretty bad luck, either getting kicked out for fighting with other band members or flouncing out just before the band had their big break. He was good-looking with a reputation as a bad boy because of his short temper and tendency to get into fights. I liked him though because of his energy and the way that he always seemed to shrug at his bad luck, never question the character defects that might have contributed to his lack of success. This made him a good drinking companion, he made me feel better about myself, never started whining at five in the morning about 'Oh I can't do this any more, oh I feel so bad about myself, oh this is such rubbish.' Buzzbreakers. I really hated them until I became one myself. Scott was always floating new ways to make money although when it came to bearing fruit, a cardboard pear on a piece of string was far more than he ever achieved.

Eva was an artist from Prague. I never saw any of her art but she told me she was an artist. When I first met her it was in a pub in the Kingsland Road and we'd done pretty much everything except jump in the bath clutching an electric fire to get a hit. Eva told me that she needed sex every day and asked if she could have the numbers of any of my male friends who might be interested in a fuck from time to time. She was quite a pretty girl in a 'lived life to the full' kind of way and she had a really nice, funny goofy smile so I was disappointed she didn't ask for *my* phone number. Afterwards, I thought that maybe it had been just the drugs talking – there are some people who seem to have a direct route from nostril to the Pandora's box of everything they've ever thought about sex ever. But in Eva's case it was true. I bumped into her a couple of days later having a coffee and she asked me quite casually if I'd dug out the numbers for her.

I didn't know that she and Scott even knew each other but about a month later, Scott and I met up to make lasagne to sell at an East London Regeneration street festival that was being run over the weekend. It was a stupid idea but I was at a loose end and had agreed to help him make the food so we went to the pub to have a couple of pints before heading back to the place where he was currently staying.

'I'm seeing this girl,' he told me over a Guinness. 'She's

crazy but a good laugh. She used to try and have sex with a different man every day until she met me.'

When we got back to the flat, which was opposite a crack den in Haggerston, I went to the fridge to start getting the ingredients together for the lasagne sauce. There was a note on the fridge which read 'Hey, babe. Look after yourself this weekend and don't get fucked up. I love you. Eva.' She had drawn a little heart in each corner of the note and it made me suddenly feel a little sad and lonely. Nobody had written little love notes on my fridge for quite some time. Ever, actually. But back then it wasn't something to which I gave a lot of thought.

'Eva?' I asked Scott as we were chopping onions for the sauce.

'That's the bird I'm seeing. She's gone back to Prague for a week.'

'Small, blonde hair, bit of a goofy smile. Czech?'

'You met her?'

'Yeah.'

I thought it was probably inappropriate to recount our conversation about her sexual needs but then Scott said,

'She's a nutter. Makes sex videos.'

'Porno?'

'Sort of, yeah. But it's alternative porno. She does them with this Latin American bird who's kind of a feminist porno entrepreneur.'

'What's alternative porno like?'

'It's like porno but done *by* women *for* women so you don't have to feel bad about it. She's got a few of them next door, I'll show you later.'

So we settled down, put on Scott's favourite Dr Alimantado CD, and started making the lasagnes. I'm a good cook and Scott had worked in kitchens before so we worked well together although we had a bit of an argument over the flour/butter ratio when it came to making the roux. But it wasn't like arguing with some idiot who doesn't know what they're doing. I despise people who can't cook, but especially men. There's something wrong with a man who doesn't know at least the basics and I don't trust them at all. I remember when I was at school and we did *Julius Caesar* and Caesar says that he wants fatties around him because they're not as untrustworthy as yon Cassius who's a devious skinny fucker. Which is fair enough although I'm not sure Mr Fatty is any more trustworthy – greediness doesn't make for loyalty either. What I would say is, get rid of anybody who can't cook because men who can't cook are sneaky, needy, manipulative types and the most likely to stick a knife in your back.

Scott and I finished off two big lasagnes, stuck them in the oven and went into the living room which was done up in a kind of cheerful Daft Punk way – little toys everywhere and fairy lights and bright plastic bits and bobs, that famously hideous painting of the woman with the blue face, a toy monkey that Scott wound up and sent around the room clashing cymbals together. He seemed to have forgotten about the alternative porno videos and I felt a bit awkward asking about them because it would look like I just wanted to see Eva with her kit off which was true but something he would take the piss out of me for. So we started having a conversation about how it was great to spend an evening making lasagnes rather than taking drugs which then turned into a conversation about how great drugs were and a couple of phone calls later everything was proceeding as you might expect.

At some point in that long evening, Scott remembered about the alternative porno videos and put a couple of them on. It's strange sitting watching pornos with another bloke, even the alternative type, because there's only one real point to watching a porno and we weren't going to do that in front of each other.

There were a couple of films – neither of which seemed to really qualify for the title 'alternative'. The most alternative, in the sense that it was utterly boring, showed Eva masturbating on a trampoline with a riding whip and was called 'The Bouncing Czech'. There was another called 'Czechmate' where she did various people dressed up as the horses and bishops of a chess set. But the one I remembered best was a film whose lame pun at least did not involve Czechs which was called 'The Twelve Lays of Christmas'. And I didn't remember that for the sex (although the Two Turtle-Doves were pretty enjoyable in a predictable male voyeur kind of way) but for a curious detail involving Eva's starring role in the Eight Maids a-Milking sequence. The task of the eight maids was pretty obvious and much easier on the eye than the Drummers Drumming or the Five Gold Rings. It was laughable stuff but there was a moment – a tiny instant – when the camera zoomed in just on Eva in her milkmaid outfit and she turned and gave that slightly cheeky, slightly goofy smile that was her trademark. And I felt quite – what's the word? – quite touched by it, quite moved.

I thought how strange it was: here was this girl who had taken the risk to move here from Prague, to make a new life for herself, to fill her world with big proclamations about her sexual needs and to fill her flat with all these kitschy toys and who made alternative porno movies directed by a Latin American feminist entrepreneur but who left little notes with hearts in the corners for her new boyfriend, stuck to the fridge. And I thought how many people there were in this strange heartless city, just floating about, all the Czech Evas and Scottish Gerrys and French Saras, all clinging on in their own way and how if I didn't hang about in bars and waste my life I would never have met them, I would never have known that smile from a TV set into a room warm with the smell of lasagne that Scott and I had just made.

It was just a moment, though. We forgot about the lasagnes and they burned but it made no difference as we were so wrecked we would never have gone and sold them anyway. We went and stood outside the supermarket for half an hour until it opened and sold us a bottle of brandy and then we saw the East London Regeneration festival which had a clown and a rap competition for the local yout 'dem and then we made a few more phone calls and didn't go to bed for four days, claiming that we'd got our new set of wings.

Scott, Eva and I hung out together for a few months and talked about all the things we would do, about writing a non-porno film screenplay together but then Scott and Eva split up because his drug habit was totally out of control while she would have quite liked him not to get so fucked up, as her note on the fridge suggested. And Eva vanished, because that's the other thing with the Czech Evas of this world: blink and they're gone. And Scott, his last plan, a plan too far, was a trip to the Caribbean, from where he was followed with a suitcase full of cocaine and nabbed at Heathrow. Had it come off, he would only – I discovered later – have received five grand for this piece of enormous stupidity. Instead of which he received ten years in prison.

'You ready, Jim?'

I turn back from the window and Hans is putting Katty's jacket on over her partridge outfit. I wonder why he didn't think of getting a taxi but maybe that would have felt just too much like submission, that little bit too humiliating.

We make our way out of their flats and outside it's a

bright, cold Christmassy night. Some of the flats across the way have been done up with flashing reindeers and Father Christmases. In the distance, the Canary Wharf tower that I can see from my own flat in the Bow Quarter is also glittering and winking. The pub is all steamed up and noisy and at one point a couple wearing purple tinsel come laughing out of the door and the girl pushes the guy up against the side of the pub and kisses him really hard. And I'm thinking what am I doing this for? Why am I trying to live this decent, sober life when some lunatic might fly a plane packed with radioactive material into Canary Wharf and kill us all anyway, when nobody is going to push me hungrily up against the wall and kiss me as a reward for all my effort, when I don't meet stupid, fearless people like Scott and Eva any more.

So the black dog of depression is biting my heels and I'm scared it might really get hold of me when suddenly I feel a little surge of fear from the two people beside me and Katty takes my hand. There's a gang of kids ahead of us – all about fifteen or sixteen – and they're laughing as they watch us approach and starting to do stupid German accents and shouting 'Kosovo Nonce' at Hans, who is looking even more terrified than his daughter. Katty starts to cry and says that she wants to go home and I think for a moment that Hans might agree with her so I take her hand and march us on until we're almost level and then one of the kids says something so stupid and ugly and horrible in that voice they've all got these days and it makes me so angry that I stop and turn.

'What did you fucking say?'

'Please, Jim . . .' Hans says and he's right because this is exactly what they want and one of the boys comes over and he repeats what he said and his little crowd are backing him up. In his hand he's got a Coke can and he starts to spill some of it on the road and it's not Coke but petrol I can smell. And he's smiling at me and in his other hand he's got a lighter.

Canary Wharf tower is blinking behind us. A couple wrapped in tinsel are kissing against the wall of a pub. The stars have been smashed out of the sky by the lights of the city.

The boy steps towards me.

Somewhere Hans is holding his daughter's hand.

What's the point of a life without trouble?

The boy is flicking the lighter.

'Do it,' I say. 'Let's see if you've got the bottle, son. But remember one thing. The second you do I'll grab hold of you and never let go. Think I'm not fast enough?'

And I step towards him.

He must see something in my eyes at that moment because he flicks a little petrol at my foot, calls me a wanker and turns back to his mates and it's like we're no longer there for them.

When we get to the school, I promise Katty I'll stay and

see her and while we're waiting and drinking tea from plastic cups and looking at the parents with their kids I've still got that pain in my heart, that ache that all started from remembering two people I used to know so long ago.

But when the pantomime starts, I go off into a little dream world and the memory of Scott and Eva begins to fade, while the strange sad calm that I can handle, that I can live with, starts to return. Katty the Partridge sits in her pear tree and the Turtle-Doves hop around and the French Hens strut and cluck. And then the eight Maids a-Milking come prancing out on to the stage with a spotted cardboard cow and, of course, one of the more enthusiastic of the maids falls over. The audience half gasps and half laughs and the child stands stunned until a teacher comes out from the wings, picks her up, dusts her face and wipes away a tear. And the kid looks out into the hall, at all the faces watching her, willing her to carry on and she smiles and leaps back star-shaped to join her friends.

Nine Ladies Dancing

Lauren Henderson

There is a fairy story which begins with a young man leaving his cottage one night to take a walk down to the nearby woods. Why he goes, the story doesn't say: to check the gamekeeper's traps for the odd rabbit, perhaps; to poach a salmon or two; or merely to wander by the river, wishing he were in love with someone.

That night there is a waning moon, still large enough to pool over the water's ridges and hollows, reflecting off the river's mirror like an arc light. And by that pale clear light, he sees a sight so strange and unexpected that he catches his breath and instinctively ducks down behind a bush, parting its stubby branches so he can watch without being seen.

Eight girls, dancing in a clearing by the water's edge. Eight beautiful girls, dancing in a wide circle, to music only they can hear. Their dresses are long, girdled at the waists with cords of gold silk, heavy with embroidery, and as they raise their arms the wide trumpet sleeves fall back from their wrists and he can see how pale they are, pale as ivory. They might never have been touched by the sun. Their skin is like skimmed milk, watery, almost translucent; he imagines that if he crept closer he could see the tracery of every vein just beneath its surface, delicate and blue.

They link their hands now, closing the circle, and, shaking their long hair back from their faces, laughing, they begin to execute a complicated series of steps, twisting in and out, moving towards each other and then away, passing underneath upheld arms and through in two winding lines without ever loosing their hold on each other's hands. Formal dancing, the kind that ladies are taught in childhood and have the leisure to practise. But the more he watches, the more he realises that there is something curiously unfamiliar about it. He's seen the lords and ladies dancing at the Great House; when he was a boy, he and the other children from the village would climb the hill on Christmas Day and press their faces to the costly glass windows of the squire's mansion to gawk at the revelry within. Velvets and silks and gold nets to hold back the ladies' hair, the latest fashions and dances fresh from the King's court in London. Tables laden with roasts and delicacies, whose leftovers would be minced up the next morning to make pie fillings for the villagers' Boxing Day party in the servants' hall.

And yet this dance is something he has never seen before. Different. Haunting. He almost forgets to breathe as he watches; he is entranced. And he begins to realise who these creatures are, and he knows he must slip away, retrace his steps home before he is trapped watching them for ever. God knows he has heard enough stories from his nan about what happens when you stumble across fairies in the woods by night.

Much as he wants to stay there till dawn comes up, he summons his resolve. Reluctantly, he moves away from the bush, still half squatting, careful not to raise his head above the cover it provides. He averts his gaze from the dancing ladies, or whatever they might truly be, and edges backwards carefully, making for the next bit of cover. And then, a little further down the rush of the river, he sees her.

She is bleached out by the moonlight, her long hair a colourless fall over her pale shoulders, her dress white as bone, the trees behind her black shadows on which her dancing throws kaleidoscopic patterns as she spins and spins around. She is dancing all alone on the bank of the river, and she seems to be moving in a cylinder of silence, her eyes half closed, their lowered eyelids white in the moonlight, her feet scattering dried leaves in a constant quiet susurrus. But there must be some kind of music playing in her head, whose changes of rhythm dictate sometimes that she slow down till she is winding her body in an endless dreamy spiral like wool turning around the spindle of a loom, and sometimes that she speed up till her toes drum the forest floor and her arms describe great geometric shapes in the air.

She looks almost as if she is skating in circles, as the villagers do on the lake every winter. He imagines her leaving figure-of-eight scratches in her wake. The other dancers were laughing, joyous, taking pleasure in the complicated patterns they were tracing with their joined bodies; but she seems lost, he thinks. Alone. He senses that she is dancing to keep herself from thinking about anything but the constant whirl of motion, the spins and loops of her feet, the arches of her spine, her arms beating the air like wings.

He realises that he has sat down on the slope so that he can watch her better. He has no fear that she will look up and see him; he can tell how completely absorbed she is by the small world she is creating for herself. Faint laughter reaches him from further up the river's edge, where the eight other girls dance in their circle, but for the most part he watches in utter silence, broken only by the sounds of her feet slapping the piles of dead leaves and the river running over its rocky bed, catching at every little jagged spar of stone as it passes.

He has no idea how long he sits there. He is in a trance now, as much as she is; if she's casting a spell on him with her dance, he is a willing victim. But somehow he doesn't believe that she is throwing out a net to ensnare any reckless fools who are careless enough to wander in the woods after dark and fall prey to the fairies. Nothing exists for her in these moments beyond the dance she's making for herself and one unexpected, entranced spectator.

Eventually, stiff with fatigue, he makes some small unwary movement that cracks a twig beneath him. In the silence, it sounds as loud as the ring of a blacksmith's hammer striking the anvil. He looks down in panic, shifting position, but when he raises his head she is gone, and it is nearly dawn.

He's bone-tired the next day, and work comes hard. Still, he doesn't spare himself. His head is so full of the girl that physical labour is a welcome relief, and all day he pushes himself harder than he's ever done before, digging trenches in the kitchen garden at the Great House, where he is an under-gardener. The housemaids giggle from the kitchen door, watching his muscles swell and bunch as he drives the spade into the hard ground. He ignores them. He has always known that a girl from the village isn't what he wants; he has his head in the clouds, they tell him pettishly, and it's true. He wants romance, adventure, a quest, not a fumble in the grass at midsummer with some girl he's grown up with and the wedding a few months later, just as she's starting to show.

That evening, the young man goes to see the village wise woman. It's either her or the parson, and, not being a fool, he has a shrewd idea about which of them will be more useful to him. He knocks on the door and waits for an answer. The firm raps he has made with her polished brass knocker echo behind the door on to the stone flags of her kitchen, fading at last into a silence in which he can hear the fast unsteady beating of his heart. More times than he can remember, he has flipped a stone across the river to watch it bound in a series of little hops off the smooth surface, like one lover teasing another with tiny kisses, until, at last, it sinks, leaving ever-widening circles to mark the spot. The circles spread until they stretch away, like a tablecloth pulled tight to flatten out the creases, and the surface of the water shows no signs that the stone has ever fallen through it. But for all that, the stone is still there, lying on the river bed, turning in the slower, heavier currents of the depths.

And that's what he thinks of now as he waits outside the wise woman's door. You do not visit the wise woman unless you want something very badly. You give her power, the power of knowing the deepest secret of your heart, something you confide to no one else. And you are frightened of the price you might have to pay. No one talks about the bargains they make with her. In return for your request, she might ask for something it will rip you apart to give. Or, even worse, she might tell you that what you want you can never have, and send you away knowing that you will spend the rest of your life longing for an impossibility.

His greatest fear is of being made to look ridiculous, a crazy fantasist, as he tells the wise woman his story. What if she laughs at him, tells him he must have been drunk last night, that the girl he saw, and her eight companions, were all hallucinations, sends him away with a flea in his ear, spreads the story of his night-time fantasies all around the village? So, as her door at last swings open, on his face can be read in equal measure the seriousness of his purpose, and, just behind it, the worst fear of all: that he might have been misled by his own senses.

The wise woman bids him come in with her customary equanimity. Indeed, being more than usually wise, she already knows why he is there, which cheers his spirits considerably. The village is scared of her, but it's a healthy respect, not the kind of fear that drives people to duck their local witch or burn her at the stake. She is careful not to provoke that. It helps that she isn't an old crone, embittered by loneliness and isolation, threatening to cast curses on disrespectful village children. Rather, she has a kind word for everyone, and has a well-deserved reputation for discretion which means that the women who come to visit her at night, begging love potions or for their wombs to be emptied of unwanted babies, can trust her never to reveal their secrets. Since she knows how to keep her own counsel, she will never be a threat to them. Which means that they will never stir up their husbands to drive her away, or worse, out of fear of what she might let slip.

If you saw her walking through the village, at first glance you would never pick her out as the wise woman. Neither pretty nor plain, neither old nor young, the only beauty she possesses lies in her long thick fall of hair, red as fresh nutmeg, which now is lightly streaked with strands of grey. But her eyes would tell you who she is, if you stopped to look long enough. You wouldn't notice the colour, or their setting; you wouldn't see the few faint crows-feet at their corners. You would see only their expression, which is serene beyond her years and tells you that this is a woman who knows more secrets than you can imagine, a woman who has heard more confessions than any priest.

She sits him down in the middle of the big wooden settle and offers him some herbal tea, which he cannot in politeness refuse. It comes in a little white cup, translucent as silk, and it is the delicate orange of infused tangerine peel; but he does not know that, as he has never seen a tangerine. He drinks it in one gulp, and asks for more. The kitchen is warm and faintly steamy. On the hob boils a pot of water out of which rises a cloud of vapour, rich with the mingled scents of clove, wintergreen, cajuput, eucalyptus, and juniper oils. Winter is approaching fast, and the wise woman does not want to catch a cold.

She pours out more tea, and the young man does the same with his heart. His life will not be worth living, he says, if he can't marry the girl. And, in her turn, the wise woman gives him encouraging news: the girl is not a fairy, fortunately enough, as that would mean disaster for him. Fairies, spirits, devils, none of them have hearts, and any human who yearns after them is doomed at least to disappointment, and at worst to damnation. The girl, however, she says – like all the girls he saw dancing the night before – is a human, snatched long ago from her family and ensorcelled by the fairies. Most of them are happy where they are; they will live for ever, never growing a day older than the age they were when the fairies took them. They sleep by day and dance by night and their recollections of their human lives come to them only in dreams, vague and hazy, implausible, clouded images of what it was like to live in sunlight, and sweat and suffer and fear mortality, dreams from which they are glad to awake, seeming to them nightmares rather than true memories.

The young man thinks of the eight girls dancing in a circle, and he agrees: this is true for them. But his girl, all alone, so isolated in her lonely dance . . . he can't believe that she is happy. He is drawn to her because she seems to need rescuing, he knows that; he wants to be the knight on the horse, riding to free the damsel in distress. But he doesn't think that this desire has blinded him so that he is imagining, or fantasising, her unhappiness.

The wise woman listens as he explains this, and she nods slowly. And then she tells him that the girl can be freed, in one way and one way only; but the way is hard, and if he fails, the fairies will have his soul. Unlike the girl he loves, there will be no redemption for him. Does he understand?

He does. The wise woman looks at him closely, looks into his heart as well as his face, and she realises that he means what he says. So she tells him what he has to do, her voice serious, its tone a warning. And she adds a proviso: she can, naturally, make no guarantee that the girl, once rescued, will choose to stay with her rescuer.

In return for her advice, the wise woman snips off a ringlet of the young man's curly hair with a small silver knife she produces from her sewing bag. A lock of hair belonging to a young male virgin, freely given it's the last ingredient she needs for a spell she's planning that will keep the energies of her lover always at their current peak. She also takes from him a solemn promise to bring over his mower every two weeks in season to keep her lawn smooth as green glass.

He leaves the house with a spring in his step, and his breath flowing through his lungs and out into the cold air more easily than he ever remembered for this time of year. He puts this sudden rush of health down to clarity of purpose, not thinking to attribute it to the tea or to the warm mist of decongestant oils, a little of which has settled on his clothing, like dew.

Three weeks later, at the next full moon, the young man follows the instructions given to him by the wise woman. He returns to the clearing where he saw the girl. At the stroke of midnight, a procession of fairies and spirits will come riding past on their way to their revels, and the girl will be among them, mounted on a horse. He must run up to her and pull her down, hold her tight, and keep looking at her, whatever happens. If he does, she will be his. If he fails, this weakness of resolve will summon up all the paraphernalia of hellfire and damnation he has been told about ever since he can remember – the parson thumping his lectern and shouting of fire and brimstone to the congregation, safe in their grey stone church on the green hillside; his mother's bedtime stories of saints and sinners, told to teach him morals and to keep him in his bed, eyes tight shut against the demons lurking around its footboard – and he will be dragged down to hell, where he will burn for all eternity. He expected nothing less.

The grass where he squats is damp and muddy. The air is icy, a wind cutting through the trees like a butcher's knife. A lazy wind, his nan would say, because it can't be bothered to go round you; it slits right through your bones instead. Rain drizzles down slowly, inevitable as winter. He welcomes the discomfort, believing, with the pomposity of youth, that he must do penance for his desires. An owl flaps slowly through the woods, the brush of its wings heavy in the night air, and disappears between the trees. A few moments later come the tiny shrill squeaks of its prey.

It sounds like the faint ringing of tiny bells. He shakes his head, confused. And then he hears the heavy thud of horses' hooves on the moist sod of the forest floor. As the first riders come into view, he sees that the horses' harnesses are sewn with hundreds of miniature silver bells, the saddlecloths velvet and dense with embroidery, the horses' manes plaited and woven with gold cord. He has never seen riches like this before in his life and he is awed by them, even though he knows that they are simply fairy magic that will vanish at the first light of dawn. He is concentrating on the horses because – apart from quick upward glances to make sure that he hasn't missed the girl – he is too afraid to look at the riders. He has flashes of terrible beauty, figures so gorgeous and unearthly that he knows he mustn't stare at them for longer than the briefest second or he will be enchanted for ever. And he sees riders who are not human at all, riders with shaggy heads like wolves who hold their reins with furred hands, and, even worse, riders who look neither human nor animal, or at least anything that he recognises: so frightening that it requires all his will and nerve to keep darting his gaze up, one horse at a time, searching, searching for her.

Finally he catches sight of her. If he needed any extra strength to do what he's resolved upon, he finds it the moment he sees her face. The other eight ladies are just ahead of her in the cavalcade, and they are laughing with each other, a beautiful, mirthful group, their horses pressed close so that their riders can whisper together and giggle over some shared joke. She, directly behind them, is as alone as ever, her face white and distant, her eyes fixed on the ears of her horse, but seeming, in the blankness of her expression, to be looking at nothing at all.

He's on his feet, running towards the girl's horse, his breath bursting out into clouds in the cold air. Around him a phantasmagoria of demons whirl, and if he looked at them his heart would stop in terror, but he only sees the girl. Her foot catches in the stirrup as he drags her down and into his arms. For a moment her eyes are the clear grey he remembers, her hair, falling over his hands, pale and straight, and then the world caves in.

She is a snake, writhing and twisting through his hands, dry and scaly, her tail throwing a noose around his neck and drawing it tight. She is a burning coal, scorching fire on to his palms, tattooing its shape for ever in blackened skin, the stench filling his nostrils and making him retch. She is a huge fish, flapping its great tail against him with tremendous force, so that he staggers back and forth trying to keep his balance and simultaneously cling on to her slippery body. She is a wolf, whose claws tear him raw and whose jagged white teeth are at his throat, ready to rip it out in a moment should he weaken his grip around its neck. He has forgotten why he is holding the shapechanger, except that he knows to let it go would be to die for certain. He remembers to look into its eyes, and the sight of the wolf's gleaming red irises so close to his makes him scream out loud in terror.

When at last, both of them exhausted from the struggle, they collapse on to the grass, gasping painfully for breath, she is again a human female, her hands sunk into his shoulders as tightly as his own around her waist, as tightly as if they were each other's lifebelts. They are too worn out to realise that now they can loosen their grip. For a long time they lie there, recovering the use of their lungs, blood flowing painfully into their torn muscles. When they open their eyes at last, they are alone in the woods. The night is slipping away, and behind the trees, the first streaks of sunlight are glimmering through the leaves.

The young man and the girl sit up and stare at each other

in wild surmise. There are many things that could happen next. They could take each other's hands; she could spit at him and run away; he could pull her towards him and kiss her as if she were his now, to do with as he liked. She has shown him the worst she can be, and he has held on through it all. Will they both realise what has happened, or will they choose to see it differently, she feeling trapped, he proprietorial?

Around his neck is a ring of bruises where the snake's tail tried to strangle him. His arms are scored deeply from the wolf's claws and the palms of his hands are blistered and red with burns. He doesn't know what to do now. Perhaps he doesn't even know if he still loves her. But, wordlessly, he turns his hands upwards to show her, like the paintings of Christ displaying his stigmata. A strangely passive gesture, to hold out his bared wrists like that, twisting them to expose the veins; an offering to be slit open with two swift flicks of a knife. And she, still staring at him, lets her gaze drop to what he is showing her. Gently she takes his wrists, curving her hands round the back of his so she does not brush the scorched and blackened skin. She takes the weight of his hands, resting on hers, and looks down at his burnt palms as if she could read their lives in them. He cannot embrace her; it would hurt him too much, and it would be strange, after they have been so close, after having her wound round him trying to claw him to death, to put his arms around her. He is still not sure that she is only a girl. But he leans forward, still letting his hands lie in hers, and rests his head, first tentatively, then with the heaviness of exhaustion, on her shoulder.

'I'm so tired,' he says. His voice is hoarse and rusty; it's hard to force the air through the bruising on his neck.

She looks down at his curly hair. Slowly she lifts a hand and traces the livid marks she has left on his skin. He flinches slightly.

'I'm sorry,' she says.

He sighs, feeling his eyes close with exhaustion. He forces them open, feeling their first words to each other should be more meaningful, better than this. Shouldn't he be on his knees in front of her, swearing eternal devotion? Shouldn't she be sobbing prettily and thanking him for her rescue? But they're both as shellshocked as two survivors of a shipwreck washed up miraculously on shore after struggling against the waves, sure they would be pulled under to their death. They have no words left. This is the reality. It is not romantic. It hurts, and they are both worn out.

He is frightened of letting go enough to fall asleep; he is so tired he knows that three slow breaths with his eyes shut and he will slip into unconsciousness. He is frightened that he will wake up to find her gone.

And then she shifts, guiding him down so his head is in her lap and he can lie more comfortably, and he curls himself around her on the ground and is asleep in the space of a heartbeat. She sits there quietly, listening to the painful rasp of his breath, and stares ahead of her into the forest, thinking of what came before this moment and what might happen after it. She imagines all kinds of different scenarios, wearing herself out with speculation. She toys with the idea of slipping back on the leaves, easing his head out of her lap, laying him down on the ground, leaving herself free. He's not sleeping so much as passed out in a semi-coma of exhaustion; he won't wake. She could stretch her legs, drink some water from the river, roam the woods, alone, truly alone for the first time she can remember. And then she thinks about how lonely she always felt before, never truly part of them but not free to leave, and she, too, realises how tired she is.

Cradling his head in her hands, she moves it away from her, just enough so that she can make space to lie down next to him. She curls around his body, breathing in the human smell, musky and strong and unfamiliar to her now after years of living with the fairies, but so comforting, almost like an animal's. She slides an arm over his waist, pressing against him for his warmth, and he moans in his sleep and shifts a little, moving back, closer to her, as she closes her eyes and lets herself slide into unconsciousness.

The sky is pale blue now, tinted with the golden-pink of dawn. A white vapour trail of a passing aeroplane skims overhead. Like all sleeping lovers, they are everywhere and nowhere. Their only reality is each other's arms.

Ten Lords a-Leaping

Jake Arnott

A discrepancy which often struck me in the character of my friend was that, although in his method of thought he was among the most well ordered of all mankind and in his manner of presenting an argument or pursuing a case or theory he was impeccably efficient, he was none the less in his personal habits one of the most untidy men that ever drove a colleague to distraction. His disorderly study was strewn with manuscripts, books and periodicals. Scattered about the room were knives, forks, cups with broken rims, Dutch clay pipes, discarded pens, even an upturned inkpot. He kept his cigars in the coal scuttle and his tobacco in the toe end of a Persian slipper. His unanswered correspondence was transfixed by a jack-knife into the very centre of his wooden mantelpiece. Everything was, one might say, 'topsy-turvy'.

His rooms reeked with the odour of the cheap tobacco that he had purchased from a small shop in Holborn, in the spirit of one of his more obscure economic inspirations. He had been taken by the slogan in the shop front that promised that 'the more you smoke the more you save' and had pointed out to me that by switching to this inferior brand he could save one shilling and sixpence a pound and, if he forced himself to smoke enough of the wretched stuff he might one day be able to live on his 'savings'. I had long since given up trying to point out the absurdity of this 'logic' to one of the greatest materialist thinkers in Europe, just as I had also given up complaining about the downright untidiness of his domestic affairs. I have become familiar enough with them to no longer take much notice of these strange habits and idiosyncrasies but in the process of introducing the young Lord Beckworth to him on that fateful afternoon (the intercession of a complete stranger forces you to renew what the first impressions are of an old friend), I confess that there was a brief moment of embarrassment on his behalf.

Yet if the young nobleman was at all taken aback by the odd circumstances of the great man, he showed it not one jot. Perhaps in deference to my colleague's reputation for mental prowess, he simply overlooked this disordered clutter, or quietly acknowledged it as one of the vagaries of genius. I do not mind admitting my own deference to my old friend as a thinker, and resent not that his powers of reasoning and deduction far outstrip my own. I am resigned to the obvious fact that he is the dominant one in our partnership and see it as my duty to assist and support his great mind without complaint or jealousy, or even much thanks from the possessor of it. Indeed, it merely falls to me to facilitate, from time to time, the practicalities needed for this prodigious consciousness to bear fruit and to keep a sober eye on the mundane matters that he all too often neglects, his thoughts, as they say, being on higher things.

It was to this end that I had, in the first instance, invited the young Lord Beckworth to my friend's lodgings. Lord Beckworth had expressed to me, when we had met earlier that year, at the house of a common acquaintance, a progressive Manchester manufactory owner, his great admiration for the work of my colleague and, more importantly, his desire to support, or even to sponsor, the continuation of his endeavours. My old friend was, at first, reluctant to be beholden to any third party in this way, convinced as he is of the need for independence in all matters. However, I managed to persuade him that he would be in no way compromised by any arrangement with this enthusiastic nobleman, and that the work itself was important enough for him to seek help from the most unlikely of sources.

Beckworth had his manservant with him, a dark, handsome looking fellow called Parsons. The conversation that afternoon started out amiably enough with the character of a harmless politeness, but very soon it became strangely weighted with a darker and more sinister nature. Formalities had been observed with a certain jocular awkwardness. My colleague made a seemingly harmless remark about social class, I think it was an attempt to include Beckworth's butler, when Lord Beckworth announced, one could almost say blurted out, as if wishing to unburden himself of a dark and terrible secret: 'Privilege, sir, is a curse!' My friend nodded and gave a vague and expansive gesture, as if agreeing that this 'curse' extended to us all, but the visitor shook his head vigorously and continued:

'No, sir, I speak not of a general curse, but a very specific one! The hereditary principle, the very fact of primogeniture that one might call a bane on the world of men, is for me a very personal scourge.'

'What?' my friend retorted, frowning.

'It is a matter of bad blood, sir. Parsons here is forever entreating me to deny the blight on my family name, but I cannot, sir.'

Beckworth looked for a moment at his manservant, who shrugged.

'Well,' said the butler slowly, 'I have always wanted my lord to find blessings in life, also.'

Beckworth smiled briefly at this, then his mood darkened once more. And, as the early evening light faded, with a foreboding he recounted, the 'curse' of the Beckworths. It was related to us that the first lord of this unfortunate house was a certain Ralph Beckworth, of yeoman stock, who had found employment in the household of James I. He was, by all accounts, a good-looking youth and he soon became one of that king's many 'favourites'. He gained his title and no small fortune, but did so without merit or breeding but rather from an exploitation of the baser instincts. Ambition, lasciviousness and a general moral incontinence that had secured him an elevated station in society, all conspired to corrupt him fully once he had attained his rank. His were the temptations of power, without the necessary moderations of genuine nobility. His debauched revels became legendary and culminated in a terrible scandal. It seems that in 1625, the first Lord Beckworth, now grown ugly and malicious in appearance, had taken a shine to a young footman in his employ and no doubt wished to make him his own 'favourite', just as he had himself been despoiled as a young man so many years before. The footman, however, was not as compliant as his master had been, but despite defending his honour with vigour, found himself imprisoned by that degenerate peer in an upper chamber of his Great Hall. Lord Beckworth and a crowd of flatterers and hangers-on sat down to a long carouse, as was the nightly custom. The poor youth upstairs was like to have his wits turned at the singing and shouting and the terrible oaths which came up to him from below, for they say that the lightest words used by Beckworth, when he was in wine, were such as might damn a man who used them. As it was, that evening there were loud declarations that he intended to exercise upon his unfortunate servant a *droit de seigneur* of the most appalling and perverse kind. The hapless footman, no doubt in utter despair at his fate, threw himself out of the upstairs window to his death on the cobbled courtyard below.

After this awful incident the first Lord Beckworth grew melancholy and brooding. He quickly developed an utter terror of high places, a vertiginous fear of falling. Not of heights so much; we know, after all, that vertigo is not the fear of heights. It is a fear of depths, of a fall. And it manifests itself not as a fear, but rather a compulsion, a desire even, for a return from the insubstantial loftiness of our aspirations, back down to earth, as it were. And it was, with this awful realisation, that the first Lord Beckworth went into a long decline, a descent into gloom and enervation. Cursed by a strange madness, he climbed up upon the roof of his Great Hall and hurled himself down.

Our young noble visitor then went on to recount the litany of his cursed family. The next Lord Beckworth had been part of the Royalist defence of the castle of Banbury, a stronghold that had been of strategic importance in the Civil War, or what my old friend would have insisted was the 'English Revolution'. In any case it seems, in a lull in the battle between Roundhead and Cavalier, the second Lord Beckworth had thrown himself, without apparent reason, from the battlements to his death.

The third Lord Beckworth had lived in exile until Charles

II was restored to the throne in 1660, and then had tripped and broken his neck on the stone staircase of Windsor Castle. The fourth lord was thrown from his horse at a fox-hunt; the fifth, a commodore in the Royal Navy, was captured by Barbary pirates and made to 'walk the plank'; the sixth fell from scaffolding whilst inspecting repairs to the Great Hall; the seventh slipped and plunged to his death from a precipice while on a walking tour of the Swiss Alps and the eighth, after an assault by footpads on Blackfriars Bridge, had been hurled into the treacherous waters of the Thames.

'And my own father,' concluded our guest, 'the ninth Lord Beckworth, was killed in a ballooning accident five years ago, leaving me this awful inheritance. The family curse is a joke to many. We are known as the "Leaping Lords".'

He gave a hollow and humourless laugh as he ended his story. I have to admit to feeling an almost disabling bafflement at the conclusion of this extraordinary narrative. My colleague maintained a more thorough and hard-headed attitude to the bewildering unravellings of this supposed 'curse'. Knowing him as I do, I observed that expression of effrontery on his countenance which manifested itself whenever he found himself confronted with any evidence, anecdotal or otherwise, that contradicted his precious materialism. His method, after all, was a method of elimination: he always sought to eliminate the impossible in order to arrive at the truth. And yet, as the street lights were being lighted that evening, I saw my esteemed friend for once on the defensive, 'on the back foot' as prize-fighters are wont to say.

'Well, your class is tainted with superstition,' he muttered, as if trying to make sense of what he had heard. 'You're, you're feudal, barbaric. I'm sorry, I don't mean this as a personal insult nor a slur on your character but just –' his gestures for a moment looked helpless, as if he was signifying the very search for meaning – 'a, a psychology, isn't that the word? Maybe this "curse" that you speak of is merely that.'

Our young nobleman merely nodded at this and the conversation quickly turned to more practical matters. He invited us both to his town house in Mayfair the following day and bade us farewell, as my friend and I had an evening appointment.

I remember feeling an absurd sense of lucidity in the artificial illumination by gaslight of the darkened streets we sauntered south into Soho for our assignation that night. The words that our noble visitor had uttered that very day still affected me deeply, their insistence reverberating in my mind with a contagious fear. I was somewhat reassured to find that my old friend, despite his abundant intellect and rationality, had been no less impressed by the strange unfoldings of the story of the Beckworths' curse.

'An interesting case,' he finally admitted as we passed through Bloomsbury. 'A series of coincidences, no doubt. But what if they were not?'

We proceeded to amuse ourselves with a kind of intellectual banter, trying to apply theories of historical materialism to what we had heard that afternoon. My friend then suggested that, perhaps, the new and controversial ideas of evolution could be related to this 'curse'.

'His class is dying out, after all,' my colleague reasoned.

'You're surely not proposing that, somehow, one branch of a social class is somehow spontaneously accelerating its own extinction?' I retorted. 'I wonder what Mr Darwin would think of that.'

'I wasn't thinking of him, but rather of the work of Pierre Trémaux.'

My friend had recently become besotted with this French naturalist who maintained that evolution was governed by geological and chemical changes in the soil and manifested itself in distinct national characteristics. I had no time for this Frenchman's far-fetched notions and did not hesitate in expressing my doubts to my esteemed friend.

'His theories are preposterous!' I exclaimed.

'No, no, not preposterous,' my colleague insisted. 'They are elemental, my dear Engels.'

When we arrived at Greek Street for a meeting of the General Council of the International Working Men's Association, our thoughts turned to the business of that evening and no more mention was made of our young nobleman and his family 'curse'. Except when one of the delegates brought up the proposal that 'All men who have the duty of representing working-class groups should be workers themselves', hastily adding with a deferential nod in the direction of my colleague, 'with the exception of Citizen Marx here, who has devoted his life to the triumph of the working class'; and my friend muttered to me: 'Well, they should have seen me hobnobbing with the aristocracy this afternoon.' But the very next morning, when we went to call upon Beckworth at his house in Mayfair, we found a police constable posted at the front door and we were informed that the young lord had died, having fallen down the stairs and broken his neck.

We were ushered into the hallway of the house and greeted by an officer in plain clothes.

'Inspector Bucket of the Detective,' he announced and took out a large black pocket book with a band around it. He produced a pencil, licked it, and ungirdled his notebook as a prelude to interrogating us both as to the movements of the young Beckworth the day before. Neither myself nor Marx has ever had much reason to trust a gendarme of any colour, particularly those who go about in mufti, as police spies and *agents provocateurs* are wont to do. But this Bucket displayed none of the underhand furtiveness one associates with such fellows. Indeed he had an altogether affable manner, if a peculiarly directed energy and purpose in his questioning. Oft-times a fat forefinger of his would wag before his face, not at us, but rather at himself as if in some form of communication. This digit seemed to have a life and intelligence all of its own and Bucket looked to it as his informant.

We learned in the course of our interview that Lord Beckworth had been found dead at the foot of the main staircase that morning by the parlour maid. The upstairs rooms were in disarray and it appeared that a great quantity of alcohol and a certain amount of laudanum had been consumed. The butler Parsons was missing and his whereabouts unknown. There was one very strange clue to the death of the young lord: a small green flower, a buttonhole perhaps, was found clasped in his hand.

Marx seemed very taken by the scientific approach of the 'detective-officer' and at the end of the questioning turned to Bucket and said:

'If I can be of any assistance in this investigation, do let me know.'

Bucket's finger twitched thoughtfully.

'I certainly will, sir,' he replied jovially. 'I certainly will.'

'Why did you say that?' I demanded of my friend when we were away from the house. 'We certainly don't want to have much to do with the police now, do we?'

'My dear Engels, I have a strange fascination with this case and feel sure I could apply my own skills and methods in investigating it.'

'But Marx, what possible qualifications do you have in the field of criminology?'

'I have spent my life trying to solve the greatest crime committed by and against humanity. Surely I can bring some of this intelligence to bear on what, in comparison, is a mere misdemeanour.'

He was, of course, referring to his definitive work on the political economy. *His* great case, if you like. But I feared that this was yet another excuse for him to be diverted from his historic task. Decades had passed since its outset and yet he had only completed the first part of *Capital*. Alas, I have grown used to so many excuses for the non-completion of the work. I had no idea why his great mind might be stimulated in pursuing this particular distraction, what was to become known as 'The Case of the Ten Lords a-Leaping', but I suggested to him that it was perhaps the supposed supernatural aspect of it that provoked him so.

'You may be somewhat affronted by the use of phantasmagoria,' I chided him. 'But wasn't it you yourself that described communism as a spectre haunting Europe?'

'Now, now,' my friend reproached me. 'Let us stick to the facts. But first let us retire into this tavern here.'

'Isn't it a bit early?'

'Yes, yes,' he whispered furtively. 'But I fear we are being followed.'

My colleague and I had long been sensitive to the attention of police spies and government agents. Once safely inside the pub there was a brief appraisal as to who our pursuer might be in the pay of. My friend was of the opinion that his movements were far too subtle to be that of a Prussian.

'You mean that he might be from Scotland Yard?' I demanded.

'Perhaps,' muttered Marx, stroking his beard thoughtfully.

'Then that is all the more reason for staying away from this unpleasant business. We must not unnecessarily provoke the attentions of any governmental institution.'

But Marx was having none of it. It has been my experience that despite his rather chaotic approach to his work, once my friend becomes obsessed with something it is invariably impossible to dissuade him from a complete involvement in it.

'Now,' he went on. 'The manservant Parsons, he seems under suspicion, does he not?'

'I suppose so.'

'And did you notice anything strange about the butler?'

'What do you mean?'

'In his appearance. Would you say he was English?'

I remember the swarthy looks of Parsons, a peculiar accent.

'No,' I replied.

'Then what?'

'Er, Jewish?' I ventured tentatively, knowing of my friend's sensitivities.

'I thought so at first, yes. But did you notice the strange tie-pin that he wore?'

'I can't say that I did, no.'

'A curious device. I've seen the emblem before. A black M embossed on a red background. I've seen it struck on medallions and tokens commemorating Garibaldi's "Thousand".'

'You mean Parsons is an Italian?'

'Yes. And I suggest that Parsons is not his real name. Here is my theory: he was a Red Shirt with Garibaldi in the triumphant success in Sicily. After the defeat at Aspromonte he goes into exile, and like so many of the "Thousand" finds himself an *émigré* in London. There he enters into the service of Lord Beckworth and adopts the name Parsons.'

'But how can any of this point to a motive in the death of the young lord?'

'I have no idea. But, as you know, it has always been my contention that it is not the consciousness of men that determines their being, but, on the contrary, their social being that determines their consciousness. I intend to discover more about this Parsons, or whatever his real name is. Once we have a clearer idea of his social interactions, then we might be able to deduce his intentions.'

He stood up from the table.

'Where are you going?' I asked.

'There is a back way from this pub. I can slip out unnoticed if you can keep our spy occupied for a while. Clerkenwell, I believe, is where most of Garibaldi's Italians have settled. I intend to make some inquiries there. Meet me at my place tomorrow at noon.'

Marx was already entertaining a visitor when I called upon him the next day, a young lady in mourning weeds. She was so shrouded in black that her face, revealed as it was beneath a veiled bonnet, seemed a half-mask of white. I do not think that I have ever seen such a deadly paleness in a woman's face. Her eyes were speckled grey like flint, her lips a blood-crimson pout. I could not help but frown when I looked from her to my friend. Marx gave a little shrug.

'This is Miss Elizabeth Cardew,' he explained. 'She was the fiancée of the young Lord Beckworth.'

'I have been informed,' she said to me, 'that yourself and your esteemed colleague here were among the last people to see my beloved alive.'

'The butler Parsons must have been the last,' I reasoned.

'That damnable fellow!' she exclaimed.

My friend and I were shocked at such an outburst and Miss Cardew's pallor was all at once infused by a rosy flush that bloomed in her cheeks. She quickly sought to regain her composure.

'I must apologise, gentlemen,' she explained. 'I'm sorry, but the enmity that I feel towards the man known as Parsons is so strong that I find it hard to moderate myself.' She sighed. 'I do believe that he had some kind of diabolical hold over my betrothed. He certainly is not the person he presents himself as.'

'Indeed not,' my colleague concurred. 'The man employed by your husband-to-be as Gilbert Parsons was, in fact, one Gilberto Pasero, a Piedmontese fighter in Garibaldi's "Thousand", forced into exile in London. He worked for a while at the Telegraph Office in Cleveland Street then, after meeting Lord Beckworth at a Radical meeting in Finsbury, was engaged in service as his gentleman's gentleman.'

Something like fear flashed in the expressive eyes of Miss Cardew.

'How did you know . . .?' she began.

'I have been conducting my own investigation. Now, you say that Parsons, or rather, Pasero, had some kind of hold over Lord Beckworth. What do you mean by that?'

'We had just become engaged when he took up with this dubious manservant.'

'When was this?' I interjected.

'Oh,' she thought for a moment. 'It was over two years ago.'

'A long engagement?' I suggested.

'Yes,' she sighed, mournfully. 'It was the curse, you see. My betrothed was terrified of it, but even more fearful of passing it on. He could not countenance the continuation of his family's bane. He had a horror that,' she gave a little sob, 'in consummating our love we might pass on something so wicked and damnable.'

She took out a handkerchief and dabbed at her eyes that were now filmy with tears.

'He always sought to try to understand his fate,' she went on. 'This led him to unconventional ideas, radical ones even. The love that I offered him seemed no consolation to his desperate temperament. Instead he seemed ever more drawn to this awful butler of his. He was enthralled in some way and I am sure that Parsons, or Pasero, or whatever this creature is really called, was responsible for my fiancé's death.'

'Have you informed the authorities of your suspicions?' I asked.

'Oh yes, but it seems that they are following procedure without much effect. This wicked manservant must be found before it is too late.'

'But where can he be?' I demanded.

'I think that I might know the answer to that,' claimed Marx.

The young lady looked as astonished as I felt.

'What?' I began.

'Just say that my contacts among the revolutionary *émigrés* in Little Italy have borne much strange fruit. Now,' he said to Miss Cardew, 'you go home. I feel sure that we will have news of this Pasero fellow this very evening.'

My friend saw the young lady out and then came back into his study.

'Now Marx,' I reproved him. 'What are you up to?'

He merely pulled out a slip of paper from his inside jacket

pocket and handed it to me. Daubed with red printer's ink on the heading were indecipherable Chinese characters and, in black copperplate below, an address in Limehouse.

We took a hansom with a good horse down to the Docks that night. A skull-like moon hung low above the river, casting a jaundiced shimmer on the dark and filthy waters below. Gaslight grew thinner, the streets more narrow, as we came closer to our appointed address. We passed gloomy brickfields, their kilns emitting a sickly light in the dripping mist. The public houses were just closing, befuddled men and women clustered in disorderly groups around the doorways. There were shrieks of awful laughter, loud oaths and raucous outbursts of brawling and disorder.

We rattled over rough-paven streets. The roads were clogged with muck and grime. The stench of putrescence hung in the air, a wraith of dreadful contagion. Most of the windows were dark, but here and there fantastic shadows were silhouetted against some dreary lamplight like magic-lantern shows of penury and degradation. Here dwelled the sordid secrets of the Great City.

'My God, Engels!' Marx exclaimed. 'Such squalor!'

I was somewhat surprised that he should be so shocked at the appalling poverty we witnessed that night. But then it always amazed me that, despite my friend's prowess in commentary and observations of conditions, his lucid approach to theoretical social analysis, he could, for the most part, be strangely inattentive and unmindful of the actual destitution that surrounds us. His detachment of thought, however, did not impair a particular attentiveness of his, no doubt born out of his many years of exile, intrigue and subterfuge, and he confided to me that he had noticed another carriage on the same trail as ours and consequently it was likely that we were once more being followed.

The hansom drew up with a start at the top of a dark lane, nearly at the waterside. The black masts of ships rose over the squatting rooftops of the low hovels. We got out and made our way towards the quayside along a slimy pavement and found a shabby house with a flickering oil lamp above the door that illuminated the same Oriental characters that were printed on the slip of paper that Marx had shown me earlier that day.

We knocked and were greeted by a sallow Chinaman who showed us into a long room, heavy with the sickly odour of opium smoke, and edged with low wooden berths, like the forecastle of an emigrant ship. The low flare of gaslights glowed feebly, their scant illumination diffused by the miasma of the foul-smelling drug. A group of Malays were hunched around a stove, clattering ivory tokens on a small table. Our attendant offered each of us a pipe. Hastily we demurred and proceeded to search amongst the stupefied occupants of the bunks on either side of us.

We were watched with suspicion by the more sober

patrons of that den. Harsh oaths were uttered as we moved through the room; one of the Malays looked up from the game in our direction and hissed something to his fellows in their alien tongue. I began to feel a concern for our safety, though Marx seemed quite oblivious to any danger, driven as always by his relentless curiosity.

'I've always wanted to see what one of these places look like,' he commented with a quite inappropriate jocularity.

Through the gloom we could make out contorted figures reclining in strange twisted poses; some muttered to themselves, others appeared to be in a trance, but all were possessed by a mental servitude to that merciless narcotic. In the corner a man lifted himself up from his bed and reddened eyes blinked against the vaporous light. He looked with a docile astonishment upon us, as if not sure if what he was seeing was real or a phantasm of his contorted imagination. He then gave a rasping and mirthless laugh. It was Pasero.

'Ah!' he called out to us. 'Comrades! Citizen Marx, now you may prove the accuracy of your aphorism as to the anaesthetising effect of religion.' He relit his pipe and taking a ghastly inhalation, held the glowing red bowl towards my friend. 'Here is oblivion, comrade.'

Marx pushed the foul object away.

'Oblivion from guilt?' he demanded. 'Is that what you seek here?'

Pasero coughed and shook his head.

'From sorrow,' he croaked, mournfully.

'Elizabeth Cardew, the fiancée of Lord Beckworth, seems convinced that you had some hold over your late master and believes that you were responsible for his death. What do you have to say to that?' demanded my colleague.

'That bitch!' hissed Pasero. 'It was her fault. It was she that drove him to his death.'

'Explain yourself, man!' Marx exclaimed. 'And why you absented yourself from Beckworth's household just after he had met his terrible fate.'

'Because no one would understand. Do you think you could understand?'

This enigmatic query was, of course, a direct provocation to the great mind of my friend. He stroked his beard, thoughtfully.

'Go on,' he insisted.

Pasero sat up on the edge of the bunk and rubbed at his sore eyes. He sighed and shook his head, as if trying to rouse his dulled mind into some sort of coherence.

'I was a young man when I joined Garibaldi's Red Shirts,' he began. 'I hardly knew myself back then. But I was drawn, I know now, to the dear love of comrades. We were a band of brothers and, through danger and action, some of us could find comfort in each other, and secretly believed in that Ancient Greek ideal: that we were an army of lovers. Ah, the Thousand! A true company of men. After Aspromonte I came here in exile, lost and alone in a cold city. I tried to involve myself in the political movements like so many other *émigrés*, but these dull meetings with their endless arguments and empty resolutions were nothing compared to the solidarity I had known with the Thousand. Then, one night, at a Chartist gathering in Bloomsbury I met with Beckworth. He was kind and generous. Although we were from entirely different worlds we were drawn to each other and we soon discovered the desire that held us in common. We shared another curse, as you would call it, like that of the first Lord Beckworth who was a king's favourite. I strove to make Beckworth see it was a blessing also.'

'You mean the abominable sin of sodomy!' I gasped.

Pasero groaned.

'Really,' Marx chided me. 'We are trying to understand the social circumstances of this case.'

'Understand gross and unnatural vices?' I retorted.

'My dear Engels,' my colleague went on, 'I would have thought that you, as the author of *The Origin of the Family*, might have a more scientific curiosity concerning this problem.'

'And encompass human perversion as part of my thesis?' I demanded.

'If you have both quite finished!' Pasero declared boldly, his voice suddenly becoming clear and emphatic. 'I am a man of action, I have little time for your analysis. You theoreticians, you have no idea what real rebellion is! We were revolutionaries of the heart, ours was the sedition of desire.'

Marx saw that I was about to make a reply to this and glared at me to keep quiet.

'We had so many plans for our liberation. Utopian ideas maybe, but we both dreamt of a world where we could be free. When we were alone there was no servant and no master but equal souls, true comrades joined together in love. But *she*!' he seethed through gritted teeth. 'She ruined everything!'

'How?' asked Marx.

'That Cardew woman's designs upon poor young Beckworth were for securing herself a social position. She preyed upon his sensitive nature and his vulnerability. When she discovered where his affections really lay she tried to insist upon my dismissal. She threatened to expose His Lordship to open scandal if he did not honour his promise to elevate her to her long-desired status as Lady Beckworth. On the night of his death she had sent him a hateful letter and a green carnation.'

'Oh that,' Marx interjected. 'What is the significance of that flower?'

'It is a symbol of our condemned nature. She wanted him to know that she knew the truth about him. He was utterly distraught, at his very wits' end. He had so much to lose. We argued, we had drunk much and taken laudanum in an attempt to quell our anxiety. We ended up fighting and in a struggle Beckworth slipped at the top of the stairs and fell to his death.'

Just then came a loud banging on the front door of the squalid den. There was a chorus of groans as the pitiful wrecks roused themselves from their berths. The game-playing Malays stood up and started jabbering at each other. After two or more heavy thuds the door was broken down and a shrill whistle pierced the night air.

'Police!' a voice called out as a group of uniformed men, with a plain-clothed man at their head, stormed into the smoke-filled room.

'Gentlemen,' the leader hailed us. 'I thought you might lead us to our quarry.'

It was Inspector Bucket of the Detective.

'But where . . . ?' he went on.

We looked to Pasero's bunk. In the commotion he had slipped out of the den through a back way.

'I've men posted outside,' said Bucket. 'He won't get far.'

We rushed out into the cold air. A figure could be seen making its way to the dockside.

'There he goes, then. And get on, my lads!' called Bucket to his men.

But it was myself and Marx that were closest to him as he reached the edge of the slippery quayside. He looked at us for a second, panting like a hunted animal, his breath steaming into the night. He gave a defiant laugh, then dropped out of sight. There was a muffled splash. As we reached the waterside we saw him flounder in the dank waters below. He struggled awhile, his body protesting against its fate, though there seemed a strange tranquillity in his countenance, as if his mind had already given up the ghost. The policemen arrived and made an attempt to drag him out of the dock with a boat-hook. But by the time he had been fished out of the dirty water he was quite cold and dead.

We gave our statements to the affable Inspector Bucket, whose curious forefinger wagged with increasing agitation at our strange testimonies. The 'Case of the Ten Lords a-Leaping' was, as they say, closed, and it seemed likely that the inquest into the death of the last Lord Beckworth would record a verdict of accidental death. A perturbing conclusion perhaps, but I must confess that our minds were reeling at the unfolding of events over the last few days. My friend's great intelligence seemed particularly vexed at all these provocations of meaning; confounded, even.

'Struggle,' he murmured to me as we made our way back to his lodgings as the dawn broke. 'It's all struggle.'

A week later I was much relieved, when I met with my colleague as he came out of the British Museum, to see that he had been coaxed back to his great work after this strange diversion. A curious-looking young man was with him who bore an intense expression on his countenance, and wore some kind of tweed hunting-cap on his head. After the briefest of formalities the young fellow left us.

'Who was that?' I asked Marx.

'Oh, a student, or, rather, he has just left university with prodigious talents and is unsure of how, exactly, to apply them. Very much like myself when I was his age,' Marx mused. 'He has lodgings in Montague Street and is using the Reading Room to develop methods of analysis. He feels sure that a scientific approach to criminology is to be his vocation. I told him of the Beckworth case and he was most interested. I believe he wants to pursue a career as a detective.'

'As a police officer?'

'No, as a civilian.'

'What a peculiar notion,' I commented.

'Yes, it's a pity that such a gifted mind cannot be persuaded to apply itself to our cause but I'm afraid he's utterly unpoliticised.'

'The youth of today,' I sighed.

'Yes. Though he is a committed materialist. It's just that he is content to analyse human behaviour and interactions without a desire to change them. Though I must confess that I can now see the fascination in uncovering evidence, interpreting disclosures and clues. One could get lost in the deduction of class and society. He is working on a puzzle presented to him by a high-born friend of his from college, a superstitious observance of an ancient family known as the "Musgrave Ritual". It is a litany of questions and answers that have no apparent meaning but—'

'Marx!' I barked at him.

He stared at me in shock for a second then his face broke into a broad grin.

'No more of this amateur sleuthing,' I reproached him. 'There's work to be done.'

'You're quite right, my dear Engels,' he assured me, patting the thick sheaf of notes he had been making for the next part of *Capital*. 'We've the greater crime to solve.'

Eleven Pipers Piping

Matt Whyman

Today, of all days, I promise not to steal. Lord knows the opportunity is out there. All those gifts in so many homes, arranged around the trees. God Himself would be in on the job, in some ways – the guy with the charisma who creates a grand distraction so I could go to work.

As a kid, I was dragged off to church on Christmas morning. If I fussed, my mother warned, all the presents would be gone when we returned home. I really believed her at the time. It would haunt me through the carols and communion. I never did go back to find the gifts had vanished. Then again, fiends like me didn't exist in those days. The kind of robbers we heard about performed casino stings or brought down banks through dodgy dealing. A family home may have been tempting to chancers, especially during the festive season, but for twenty-four hours it seemed that even thieves spent time with their loved ones. They had standards, and that is something I still believe in no matter how far I've fallen.

I didn't just remind myself of this. Last night, I looked my Mary in the eyes, and swore to her that I would not make hell for anybody. Poor Mary. I would carve out my heart for her, but that's about the only thing I can offer. Even the squat is no longer the love nest we had created for ourselves. Then again, that's the property market for you when it comes to street-level living.

At first we had the run of the building. Now we have just this single room on the top landing. It isn't filthy as you might expect. We have trinkets from our time together, worthless to anyone but us, while my collages hang in picture frames made from foil and coloured glass. We've even adopted a cat. He likes to stretch out on the ledge in the winter sun, or sleep on Mary's lap when she's on the tail end of a hit. I suppose a cat would be drawn to our way of life, given that we exist to go wild or curl up in a ball. So when I told Mary of my pledge, I was ready for her to freak out at me and ask what the hell I was thinking. Instead, she smiled bravely and assured me that everything would be OK. Even if we had nothing but cigarettes, we would get through the day.

'I wish I had your confidence,' I said. 'Just thinking about it makes me panic.'

'You need a special place,' she advised me. 'Somewhere no harm can come to you.'

'I don't have one.'

'Everyone does. Just close your eyes and take yourself there.'

When it came to dealing with her dependency, Mary was an example to me. A functioning crack-cocaine addict, that's how she seemed, and one who could count on an asset that guaranteed an income when times got really tough. I have tried to sell myself, of course, but with little reward. My magpie eye is why I gave up on that game, for it earned me nothing more than broken ribs and missing teeth. I could sink to my knees and reach for that zip as negotiated, only for my fingers to move round to my punter's pockets. I just couldn't help myself, and that's when all hell would break loose. We don't speak about our different trades, though. With no job satisfaction, it's only the cash that counts. I may have been rubbish as a rent boy, but I understood the game. As a common thief, I quickly learned that sometimes it was best not to stir up questions about where the money had come from.

How I screwed up is the story of my life, or the final chapter before the pages started falling out. We're not talking trash here, either. I'm a Barratt Home boy gone bad, and boredom was my downfall. My middle-class credentials don't invite much sympathy, but then why should a drug habit come out of a crisis? I was *underwhelmed* by life, not underprivileged, but still washed up on the same shore. What possessions I could sell were long gone, and so I turned to other people's stuff. You could see me coming, if I tried to con my way into your home. Even old ladies wouldn't let me in to read their meters any more, and who could blame them? I am skin and bone, with a hungry-looking face and some bad black tattoos peeping from my collar and cuffs. Sometimes, however, I look at myself and wonder exactly what it is that I'm trying to cover up.

Only Mary can see beyond the markings that have grown with my troubles. She even shares the same ring of thorns inked around her wedding finger. Many couples with our kind of habit lose interest in each other, but not us. Crack is what brought us together in the first place. That's why I don't blame her for being in this situation, and she does not blame me. We are enslaved to each other, and that's how it should be. Even the thought of being away from her for too long leaves me cold. Sometimes I wonder how things would be should we both succeed in getting clean. I dream about the places we'd go at last and all the things we'd do together, and then I worry that perhaps that's when we would drift apart. Our lives are lousy, looking from the outside in, but we were on a high together. Mary was my angel and my devil. She looked like a million dollars to me. All of it in dirty money, but every note counted in my eyes. My girl was golden brown, from her skin to her hair and her personality. We wanted the same things as well, which amounted to love and other drugs. One without the other just didn't deliver the fix we needed, as I would come to discover come this special day of days.

'You know what?' I opened my eyes, abandoning the void I had found with a proposition for Mary. 'We should make tomorrow our gift to each other.'

We were lying on the bed at the time, recovering from the final rock in our possession. It was growing dark outside. We had yet to switch on the light. Time, it always seemed to me, had been ticking without us, and now Christmas Eve was almost over. At once Mary was up on her elbows, peering down at me.

'Our only gift?' she asked.

Immediately I sensed I might've said the wrong thing. Her eyes narrowed, the disappointment in them turning widescreen. I tried to look away, but she had already seen right through me.

'You were hoping for more, right?'

'From a burnt-out romantic like you,' she said next, dropping out of nowhere to kiss me on the lips. 'I would expect nothing *less*.'

*

I have been awake now since dawn. I'm lying in bed, one hand in my hair, staring at the ceiling. My throat is in a bad way, as ever, like a stairwell after a fire, but all I have to inhale here is air. I will not steal today, I whisper hoarsely to myself, over and over again. Mary is still asleep, curled away from me. I'm surprised my mantra hasn't disturbed her. Then I wonder if perhaps she's wide-eyed on her side of the bed, brooding over what she's doing with a man like me. A man who can't even get it together to drum up a half-decent present! I'm appalled at myself, but that's nothing new. Every day I wonder what on earth *I'm* doing with a man like me. Whatever happens, though, I will not steal. I will not rob on Christmas Day. In the distance, I hear bells strike six times. Mary doesn't stir, and so I decide to fill my time constructively.

It's cold outside, but bright and blue. Vapour trails score the sky, reminding me of what I am missing. Normally I can keep a lid on my itches and twitches until mid-morning, but this is no ordinary day. I will not steal, I remind myself once more, but I have a plan and hope to hell it's going to work.

I arrive outside a door that has been kicked in more times than opened. Really it's just a thick block of plywood held in place by steel bolts and hinges. I give it three knocks. After a second or so, as is the only way to gain access to this place, I follow it up with another four.

'It's me,' I call out, on hearing movement in the hall, for everyone knows who I am.

'All crack fiends say that.' The voice is sleepy but gruff. 'Which "me" would that be?'

'Mary's boy,' I say, a little hurt.

'The kid?'

'I'm twenty-one, thereabouts!'

'You were nineteen, last time I asked.'

'So what does that tell you about my loyalty?' I sound desperate, but everyone expects that so it's second nature to me now.

'Prove it's you, Mary's boy.'

'What can I say? You're the lowest dealer in town with a reputation for cutting your gear with salt crystals. You even sold me a twist of bug powder one time and didn't deny it when I got discharged from hospital. Now because you're this low, I'm hoping it means you're also prepared to see me on Christmas morning.'

I hear him clear his throat, and then scratch some part of himself.

'Go home to your family,' he croaks eventually. 'Most probably they're thinking about you, this day.'

'But you *are* family to me,' I plead with him. 'In a way.' At last I hear the bolts shoot back. When the door opens, I know for sure that I have woken the dead. 'Seasons Greetings, Vincent.' I shrug and smile, puffing hot breath into the air. 'Did Santa visit?'

'Sure he did.' My dealer is an intimidating presence, even when he's dressed in a vest and tight fitting Y-fronts. Vincent is a broad-shouldered man. That, or his head is unusually small. It all depends on how you view him. Then again, the look he shoots me now leaves me feeling about six inches tall. 'Old Nick stopped by for some mince pies and ice, if that's what you want to hear.'

'Father Christmas is on crack?' I smile to myself. 'Now there's a thought.'

'What have you got?' he asks me now, adjusting himself with one hand and a tilt of his hips. 'A small rock is ten pounds. Seeing that it's Christmas Day, I'll do you three for twenty. Seeing that you've also just woken me up, I'm withdrawing the special offer. So that's ten pounds. Take it or leave it.'

Vincent is the oldest crackhead on the block, and deals to feed his habit. He was on the rocks before his career and then his family went the same way. Not that you want to give him too much rope to dwell on this. When he isn't being hard to please, Vincent is prone to tears and in need of a good hug. Twice now I've got my shoulder damp and the life almost squeezed right out of me, but it's worth it for the free pipe that follows so my man here can get a grip. This time, however, as I tell him now, I am here with a proposition of my own. It's one I'm hoping he won't refuse. For Mary's sake as well as my own.

'Do I have any odd jobs that need doing?' Vincent chews on my offer, eyeing me now like he's missed out on the punchline. 'Are you trying to be funny?'

'I need the money.'

'You're a thief. Do what you're good at. Fill your boots.'

'Please don't say that. I just want to make Mary happy with a present, but not if it makes someone else miserable today.'

I feel my cheeks heating, and look to the space between my feet.

'There's no shame in making someone happy.' Vincent says this in a whisper, and I feel a hand fall on my shoulder. I look up, pleased that I have won him over. Then his eyes turn glassy and I worry about what this means. Christmas is for family, after all, and here we are dwelling on everything he has lost. Even so, I can't afford to back out now. If I do then I'll go into remission, and I'd rather give up the ghost than steal on this day of all days.

'How about I do the washing up?' I see a tear forming in the corner of his eye, and quickly steer my attention around him. Sure enough, every surface is hidden by crockery and the hob is a disgrace from the kind of cooking that goes on in a place like this. 'Let me loose on it, Vincey. For a fiver, that's all. Then I'll leave you in peace.'

I face him again, expecting a flat refusal, and my heart skips when he says, 'Three pounds for the dishes *and* you mop the floor.'

'That's a hard bargain.'

'What do you expect from your dealer?' He tries to blink back his tears, but that just makes them spill over.

'Done,' I say, and spread my arms so he can walk into them. 'Merry Christmas, man.'

*

The kitchen sink takes a few minutes to clear before I can even fill it with suds. I hear myself saying 'These plates won't wash themselves' and feel some sense of pride when I reach for the final pot. I think about what I'm missing constantly, but don't crave that fix as much as I had feared. I'm also in a sweat, of course, but it's hot for a change and prickles for all the right reasons. After Vincent broke down on me I had half expected him to stoke up a pipe to share. Instead, he had decided to clean up with a shower, which left me no choice but to do the same over the kitchen sink. I wonder if his tears are among the muffled patter of water I can hear upstairs, and hope in time I don't end up losing the only thing that matters to me. Mary is uppermost in my mind, in fact, until I hear three knocks at the door. I freeze, thinking this would be a bad time for a bust. Then come another four knocks.

'Vincent?' I hold my breath, hoping to pick up on some sign that he has heard, but the shower continues running. I reach for the drying-up cloth and turn it in my hands. My dealer dumped his keys on the surface here before heading upstairs, and I'm not sure if I can leave them alone. Whoever it is outside calls for him by name next, but it doesn't sound like a raid. When the police come knocking here they tend to do so with a battering ram, and so I decide to do my new employer a favour. This one from the kindness of my heart.

*

'Hey! It's Mary's boy. How you doing, kid? Why you here? Did she kick you out on this special day?' The three wise guys at the door are each clutching a brace of compact discs. I can be pretty sure every last one has been stolen to justify their visit. The facial hair on them tells me they're beyond trying to hold down jobs like so many I know. They all look like castaways from their former lives, whatever that might have been. 'Is she here?' one asks, looking hopeful all of a sudden.

I tell them Mary is still asleep, and ignore the comment about her being all tired out.

'Vincent is taking a shower,' I add. 'It's dirty work, dealing with you people day in and day out.'

'True enough.' This is the second of their number. I've seen him before, lolling around a pipe in Vincent's front room. I've seen them all, I realise, when I think how many times I've been here myself. He shows me the haul in his arms. I see some criminally easy listening, and wonder who has been the real victim in this set-up. 'We were in the neighbourhood,' he tells me next, looking a little uncertain about his story. His buddies don't appear too comfortable either, standing on the street with white hot goods, but I'm just not sure I should let them in. 'Everyone knows how Vincent can get a little emotional on special days, so we just thought we'd drop by with some presents.'

'How thoughtful,' I say, and raise one eyebrow. 'Gifts for your dealer, huh?'

'Will you just let us in?' This comes from the one who's been so silent. His attitude could use some softening, just as that beard could benefit from a trim. He steps up square to me, chapped lips curling. Then his eyes find the damp drying-up cloth slung over my shoulder, and that snarl becomes a goofy smile.

'What are you today, his bitch?'

'That's none of your business,' I say, but it doesn't sound too good. 'OK, I'm helping him out for money, is all.'

'Uh-huh.' All three of them nod like they don't believe a word I say, and this becomes quite clear to me when Vincent appears at my side, pulling tight on his dressing-gown cord.

I leave Vincent to negotiate with these berks in the front room, while I finish off the kitchen with a mop. I'm burning up at what was just read into the situation, and try hard to remind myself why I'm here. I will not steal to find this money. I will not rob on Christmas Day. I squeeze shut my eyes for a moment, hoping Mary's words of wisdom might conjure up somewhere in my mind that will help me out here. Once again, however, I just can't shut out what I want most of all. A rock right now would take care of my feelings. It doesn't help that I can smell them cooking from here, and yet there's nothing in this kitchen that will take care of my growing hunger.

'Knock, knock, little bitch.' I spin around, mop in hand,

to find the guy with the tapered beard filling the doorframe. He's toasted now, shifting his weight from foot to foot, and that just makes me all the more mad. 'Vincent has been telling us you're planning to surprise your girl.'

'So I am,' I say. 'But I'm not carrying any cash yet, if you're planning on shaking me down.'

He shows me his palms, says: 'What do you take me for?'

'An addict,' I say. 'You're no different from me, and I'm damn sure I know what I'd do in your shoes, if it wasn't for this day.'

'This day,' he repeats under his breath. 'Makes you think, times like now.'

The moment that follows is marked by the sound of sobbing. It's coming from the front room, and explains why the other two crackheads appear looking just as wired but equally sheepish.

'What happened?' I ask.

'Vincent,' they chime together, like that explains everything.

I sigh, and move my mop around the floor once more. 'A hug would've helped him out, guys. It certainly would've meant more than your "gifts". Now will you clear out of here? I have work to do.'

They turn to leave, only for the one who first came to me to pause for a beat. He glances back, and then comes around full circle.

'You know, maybe we really should do something special.

Some decorations. And a tree. Yeah. With lights and tinsel.'

My eyes slide to his two mates, but it's clear from the way they both shrug that he's gone off on this one alone.

'With lights and tinsel?' I repeat, to check I heard him right. His unblinking eyes don't tell me whether he's just too shot through for his own good, so I try to humour him into talking some sense. 'D'you think a fake tree or real?'

'I don't *do* fake, man. Norwegian fir is the only tree fit for a front room. Doesn't matter where you are, a proper tree can make a place feel like a palace. Even a dive like this.'

As he paints his picture, the two guys behind him begin to look up and around. Had I been primed like them, I'd be right there as well. As it is, I see a way out of my own fix, and nod encouragingly.

'You need balls,' I add. 'To hang from the tree, I should say.'

'Damn right we need balls. Big silver ones. And a string of flashing lights.'

'How about some of that spray-on snow?' the second guy chips in. 'My old mum used it for the windows.'

'Does it come in an aerosol?' I know the answer, but figure sowing this kind of seed among drug desperadoes can only produce a bumper harvest.

'Snow,' the main man says to confirm. 'We definitely need fake snow.'

'Good call.' I'm all fired up myself as Vincent shuffles into the kitchen to join us. He's clutching a vodka miniature with the bottom cut out, but it's his eyes that tell me he's just been sucking on the *devil's dick*. I look at him good and decide what he really needs isn't another rock for his pipe but a paper party crown. So I stand up straight once more, braced now to close this deal. 'Let me take care of everything,' I suggest, and beam broadly when our dealer is persuaded to fund it.

That afternoon, I leave with a clear profit and the chance to make Mary's day. All the festive gear had come from my fence, and paid for with the money I had been entrusted to spend wisely. I even brought the fence back with me, and half a dozen other crack-cocaine disciples who had been at his flat at the time. None of them were strangers to Vincent, and before their first pipe could be prepared we all worked hard to get the paper chains in place so the room looked like a place to have a good time. We shifted back what was left of the sofa, rearranged the chairs to create more space, then laid out nibbles and paper cups. With the tree up, and the lights glittering, the place seemed way more inviting than ever before. I kept my head straight throughout, though it nearly killed me to pass on the first hit. All I wanted was to be in one piece when I next saw my girl. Plus I had agreed to warm the mince pies as part of the package and I missed out on the second pipe. By the time I walked into the front room with a laden plate and a parlour game in mind, I found eleven crack-cocaine slaves in the highest possible spirits. Vincent seemed the happiest of all. He was jabbering away at anyone who would listen, so I extinguished the cigarette that was threatening to burn the webbing between his fingers, and told him it was time for me to head home.

'You go,' he said between sentences, and got it together to peel out a ten-pound note for me. 'That's three for the kitchen. Seven for the party planning. Are you sure you don't want any candy now you can afford it?'

I told him no, folded the money into my back pocket, and then hurried away like all the oxygen in the room had threatened to run dry.

I let myself out, aware that I was leaving the place unlocked, and took a deep breath. Normally, Vincent would've been right behind me with his big keys, but not this time. Addicts could be funny like that. Some days, they bolted themselves away from the world. Other times they got so loaded that security fell apart because the world didn't exist beyond their front door. I crossed the road with my head down, out here in the cold. I was walking away from my dealer's house with a clean head and an ache I couldn't shake. Somehow it just seemed wrong, leaving with money instead of rocks. Every step grew harder, the more I brooded on it, while the chill continued to build. It was as if Vincent had sunk a fishing hook between my shoulder blades when I turned my back on him. I could see him in my mind's eye now, searching inside his pocket for the bait that would reel me in. And I had enough cash in my pocket to pay for it. I had money to *burn*.

'Damn it,' I muttered to myself, for I had come so far. 'Damn it all.'

I drifted home a little later than planned. The squat no longer had a door to leave open or lock, just a sheet of corrugated metal that you had to curl at the corner to squeeze through. The way it had been dog-eared told me that the last person through was still inside, but it made no odds to me. People came and went from here at all hours. In fact, as I made my way to our landing I passed some guy on the stairs. I hadn't seen him here before, and he certainly didn't look like he wanted to be remembered. I moved aside as he came down, expecting a glance or a nod of thanks, but he was too busy ignoring me to notice. I shrugged to myself, and headed into our room to find the only person that mattered to me.

Mary had only just slipped out of bed, it seemed, judging by the sheets. I joined her at the window. She was dressed in an old sweatshirt of mine that she hadn't been wearing before, with her hair tied up in a topknot. I stood beside her for a moment, looking out at this crisp, still day, and then she faced me squarely. My girl was all made up, and not just to see me. I was going to speak, but the words I had in mind just fell apart.

'Happy Christmas,' she said, and took my hand. 'It's been tough, sorting out a gift for someone who has nothing.'

I felt her press something into my palm. I knew what it would be just by closing my fingers around it. A ten-pound deal just like the one I had for her. If she was surprised when I pressed the very same thing into her hand then she hid it well. She didn't even ask how I came by the money, and I had no intention of asking the same thing of her. If Mary shared my love and devotion, the question was totally insignificant. That it was left unspoken meant more to me than any story we might've spun for each other. I could've told her I had prepared a party in a crack den, just as she might've said she found her money in a shoe. It was just too good to be true, coming from two junkies, and so we left it at that.

'Happy Christmas to you, too,' I said, wishing now for nothing more.

We kissed, passionately, both of us clasping what had to be the most perfect presents ever. For these were gifts we could share to forget about this godforsaken day, here in our own special place.

Twelve Drummers Drumming

Patrick Neate

Miss T thinks she can see more with her one eye than most people do with two. Sometimes she thinks she can see everything. Perhaps this is how she can sit on her wicker chair outside her front door for hours at a time, endlessly fascinated.

She is there for the early morning rush hour when the air is crisp and the whole street perfumed with the scent of a thousand hurried baths, and she notes the light footsteps of the ambitious and the laboured shuffle of those close to breaking. She is there for the procession to school and, among the smart navy uniforms, she observes the budding personalities – the swagger of the show-off, the anger of the bully and countless other characters besides. She is there when the drunkards make their way to and from their watering hole and she recognises those with reason to drink and those whose reason has long been lost. She is there when the gangsters take up position at the signpost on the corner and she watches the self-conscious vanity of their every gesture that betrays the confidence of their narrow gaze.

Miss T likes to say, 'Open eyes see only so much. An open heart sees everything.'

She says this to the old women who pause to rest with her on the way to visit their sons and daughters or as they head home from the market. They are not her chosen companions – they are simply the only ones to stop – so she is not surprised that they don't understand. Typically they respond to her with a shake of the head and some long-winded story about how things are different these days and nobody is open-hearted any more.

Miss T doesn't agree but she doesn't say anything either. She sees that these old women regard her as one of their own with her eye patch, stooped posture and hair the colour of ash even though, in fact, she is only forty-two years old. She sees too that the older generation need to regard the past, however terrible it may have been, as the era when everything was done properly and well. After all, this was their time just as, however fleetingly, it was hers.

What Miss T means by her statement, however, is this. She believes it is possible for a single event to break open your heart so violently that you can never close it again.

When this happens your heart is permanently exposed and then you can't help but see the happiness and sadness, the hopes and fears, the inspiration and repression of every person you encounter. You are like a medium who cannot control the spirits who possess your soul whether helpful or bitter. You are like a bank vault that accepts the deposits of honest customers and corrupt businessmen alike. You are like a split pomegranate whose ruby flesh tempts both a hungry child's soft mouth and the beak of a greedy bird. This is how Miss T feels.

A short lifetime ago, before she felt like this, Miss T learned the English word that describes it perfectly. 'Empathy'. She likes this word and sometimes when she sits on her own she says it softly to herself and enjoys the ways it makes her lips and tongue move. There is something sensual about it, as if it were a kiss or a declaration of love. She thinks this is entirely appropriate. Miss T sees everything and therefore cannot be surprised by anything. She knows that this state has made many others who suffered as she did bitter or corrupt or greedy. But her? She simply feels open and therefore unwilling to pass judgement on any character or action. This is empathy and isn't there something innocent about it, even though it derives from experience? And, you see, 'innocently' is the only way she has ever felt love. It happened just once. And that was a short lifetime ago.

As for the hurrying workers, eager students, hopeless drunks and vain gangsters that pass Miss T's front door . . .

all those pairs of eyes rarely see her. In fact, the only time they seem to notice her at all is at twilight when her figure is illuminated by the glow from the rubbish tips that are burned a little way behind her matchbox house. Then some passers-by stop and squint and stare at her motionless silhouette with its blazing outline and they cover their mouths and noses against the smoky air and wonder who she is and, perhaps more, who she was.

By the time Thandi turned fourteen with the new year of 1976, she was a studious and precise child. Her ankle socks were neatly turned up, her hair in different styles but always just so and her exercise book carefully covered in newspaper to protect its binding. She did her homework the day it was set, recited multiplication tables as she walked to school and read whatever she could get her hands on – a dictionary, a romantic novella, a battered magazine – late into the night. Sometimes her father would come into the girls' bedroom and insist she extinguish the paraffin lamp. Then Thandi would be forced to use up one of the precious candle stubs she kept by her bed and she read until her eyes hurt or the light finally flickered and died. Sometimes she even read when she was supposed to be preparing the evening meal. Once, when the pot boiled dry, her mother, Marcia, scolded her. 'What is so interesting that you forget the cooking? We can't eat words, you know.'

But Thandi replied, 'Not yet, Mama. But I have the chance to learn and that will lead to other opportunities in the future. You'll see.'

Thandi thought she was lucky. After years of precious little money for the local schools, the government had recently begun to invest and more and more places were now available. This was how she was the first in her family to be able to attend school.

Thandi's father thought her education a waste of time; at least that's what he said. Although christened Cephas, he was known as 'Taxi' to everyone, even his wife, because that's what he'd driven for more than twenty years and he heard a lot of opinions and he brought some of them home. 'Why does the government build schools?' he used to say. 'Why does a man train a donkey? Because he wants it to work for him, that's why.'

Nonetheless, Taxi privately supported Thandi's studious nature, albeit for two reasons of his own.

The first reason was that he recognised it was Thandi's love of school that had overtaken her other great passion: dancing. His wife said that before Thandi had learned to walk, she'd learned to dance, clapping her hands and waving her arms at the sound of any radio outside the house. Indeed Marcia claimed that, as an infant, her daughter had been able to find rhythm in anything, from the sounds of clothes being scrubbed to the choke of a car engine on a cold morning.

Now Taxi had no problem with dancing itself but if it were ever combined with his second reason he could see plenty of troubles ahead.

The second reason Taxi supported his daughter's study, you see, was this: he knew that she was changing. Each morning when he met her at the breakfast table, he felt he should rub his eyes in astonishment and he could barely bring himself to look at her. What had happened to the spindly little girl with pencil limbs stuck on to a body plump with puppy fat? In her place was a young woman with hips and a round backside and the outline of a full bosom suggestive against the white material of her school blouse.

And Taxi wasn't the only one to notice the changes. Sometimes when Marcia sent Thandi on an errand, he stood at the door of his house and watched her go. He saw the working men, heads bent in exhaustion and buried in the neck of their overalls, suddenly look up as she passed. He saw the young gangsters who hung out on the streets suck their teeth and shout out to her and it took all his self-control not to call her back.

The only person who didn't seem to have noticed that his daughter was now of an age and dimension to attract attention was Thandi herself. Taxi put this down to her obsession with studying. Imagine if she'd still loved to dance now that she looked like this? It didn't bear thinking about.

Of course parents rarely acknowledge their own offspring's precocity and the truth was that Thandi was well aware of the way men now looked at her and, what's more, she still loved to dance. But she was sensible enough to know that the men who were interested in a girl her age were dangerous and she limited her dancing to just once a week.

Every Saturday afternoon, Taxi would head down to the local beer hall and typically, a couple of hours later, Marcia would have to send Thandi to fetch him home. Thandi never went into the beer hall and sometimes she gave a message for her father to one of the other customers. But usually she preferred to just wait around in the shadows outside. There she met other local children and they soaked up the heady sights and sounds and bathed in the honey-thick atmosphere. They loved to watch the notorious gangsters who looked so smart in their chalk stripe suits, they thrilled at the sight of the prostitutes in their brash, colourful dresses and they laughed at the beer-soaked drunkards who stumbled out into the darkness.

Most of all, however, they were enchanted by the booming music that leapt out of the beer hall from the radio within and filled the night air: all sorts of styles but all made for movement. They whooped with delight at a familiar tune and then they danced, girls together and boys alone, swinging their hips and jitterbugging their feet, their expressions locked in something like rapture.

It was on an evening such as this that Thandi first met Sam. She'd seen him before of course – he'd started in the form above her with the new school year – but they'd never spoken. Then, one night, he was outside the beer hall with his two older brothers. They each had a drum and they sat on the steps and began to snap out beats that syncopated with the sounds of the music inside.

The three were all skilful but Sam was the best and momentarily Thandi was frozen by the sight of this boy whose hands worked that drum skin like raindrops on a window. In spite of herself, she found that she was considering him as if from a great distance. There was a seriousness in his face that belied the joy in his activity, as if he was a deep thinker who could express himself only in rhythm. Perhaps if she'd had a little more experience, she'd have realised that she thought they were two of a kind. But she was just a girl and when that realisation finally arrived it was much too late. Suddenly – standing there, watching – Thandi's heart seemed to sync itself with the complex sounds rapped out on Sam's drum and she began to dance. She danced like she never had before – joyful and abandoned but also, for the first time, with the same intensity she applied to her studies.

By the time Taxi finally emerged of his own accord, she was dripping with sweat and she briefly ducked into the shadows to gather herself. Before she went to greet her father, however, she felt she had to say something to the young drummer. She touched him on the shoulder as he played and he looked up without stopping.

'I'm Thandi,' she said. 'We're at the same school.'

Still the rhythm cracked and bit. He smiled at her and his teeth and his eyes were clean and white. 'I know,' he said. 'I noticed you first.'

It was that night when she went to bed reading her dictionary that Thandi came across the word 'empathy'. And before she'd drifted off to sleep, she'd learned 'enamour' too.

Although it is winter Miss T still takes her place daily in her wicker chair outside her front door. She wraps herself up in her thick woollen blanket, adjusts her eye patch and she watches.

One afternoon she is joined by Mama Sylvia and they share a pot of tea. Sylvia has a broad, puffy face with small eyes like two tiny pieces of coal deep-set within her fleshy cheeks. She also has an unlikely voice that is high-pitched, reed thin and curiously genteel and anglicised.

Among all the old women who come and sit with Miss T, Sylvia is the worst for talking about the past as a superior place. This, that and the other were all, she says, better when she was a girl. Although Miss T understands that Sylvia is now frightened by the present, she still has to hide a smile behind her tin mug. Of all the nations in the world to adopt rose-tinted nostalgia, she thinks, this is surely the most ridiculous.

When Sylvia has finished speaking, they sit in silence for a while. The homeward school procession begins to pass. Gangs of hearty young boys, their ties loose on their chests or looped around their foreheads, run by, play-fighting and whooping and showing off. The girls amble more slowly. They hold hands and giggle, their uniforms still just as neat as they were that morning.

Then a car pulls up. It is a bright yellow BMW with tinted windows and Miss T recognises it immediately as belonging to one of the local gangsters. Four young men get out, laughing and joking. They are peacocks, dressed in baseball caps, loose jeans and colourful, logo-heavy T-shirts, with dark glasses hiding their eyes and heavy gold chains at their necks. The car's stereo system is booming the latest local hits and some of the schoolgirls glance shyly at these street thugs while others stop and smile, brazenly flirtatious. The young men cock back their heads and whistle through their teeth. Two of them start to dance, beckoning the bravest schoolgirls towards them.

Now Sylvia stands up and bustles to the side of the road. She wags her finger at the gathering group: 'You! I know you criminals and drug dealers! Why do you want to bother decent people with this rubbish?'

One of the gangsters cups his hand over his ear as if he is straining to hear then he ducks his head into the car and turns the volume up another notch. Two of the others start to laugh, which gives the cheekiest schoolgirls the licence to do the same. But the fourth member of the crew seems more uncertain. He looks momentarily embarrassed and he can't take his eyes off Miss T who is still sitting, unmoved and placid, in her wicker chair, though now a beaming smile is broad across her face.

Sylvia glances back to her companion, shaking her head. 'Boys like this!' she exclaims. 'They have no respect any more!'

Miss T says nothing. She doesn't think this is true. Or at least she sees that the younger generation need to believe they are on the cusp of something better. After all, this is their time and, just for a moment, she can remember how that felt.

This situation could get out of hand. Sylvia strides towards the car and attempts to reach the stereo herself. One of the young men blocks her way and, although he is still grinning, he takes off his shades and his eyes are hard and his mouth spitting curses. But for once Miss T doesn't notice any of this. Her one good eye is fixed on the fourth young man who returns her gaze. She slowly stands and switches her attention to the dancing schoolgirls and their quick feet that stamp out a tattoo in the dust. Their steps take her back to her childhood as if this dance has been unbroken for the best part of thirty years.

It was through Sam that Thandi became involved in the student movement. Of course she'd known about it before but she'd never thought to take part since she was top of her form and didn't want to do anything that might disrupt her schooling. Then she began to listen to Sam's forthright opinions.

'You can work hard, pass all your exams and find a good job,' he said. 'So what? You'll be one of the finest monkeys in the zoo but you'll still be waiting for the keeper to feed you.'

Thandi laughed: 'You're starting to sound like my father.'

As it turned out, though, Taxi was distressed when he discovered his daughter's new interest in politics. He took her to one side and spoke in a whisper as though someone could be listening. 'No good will come of it,' he muttered. 'When you were a baby, we sang "free in '63". Imagine! And now look at us here in 1976. The situation is worse than ever.' But by this time her father's was no longer the male opinion to which she paid most attention.

After their first meeting outside the beer hall, Thandi and Sam started to spend more and more time in each other's company. All their schoolmates assumed they were boyfriend and girlfriend. But they weren't; not at first. They simply shared the same interests.

Like Thandi, Sam was a serious student who had little patience with anything he considered 'childish'. What's more, in March of that year, Sam and his two brothers founded a group of drummers at the school. The group was a dozen strong and they practised in the yard at break and after the final bell. They called themselves Meadowlands

Beat and their every rehearsal attracted many of their fellow students who would dance to those syncopated rhythms for as long as they played until it was like a daily competition between the group and their followers to see who would tire first. A pattern emerged in which Thandi was always the last dancer dancing and Sam the last drummer drumming while the others were doubled up panting or prostrate and laughing or simply cheering them on.

At the end of every session, Thandi and Sam would walk home together. Sometimes they talked about their respective classes, sometimes politics and sometimes music. Sometimes they were silent. Sometimes Sam would reach for her hand and hold it tight. His fingers were thick and strong and calloused. Once he kissed her. It was after they'd been arguing over some or other political issue.

Though she didn't mean to, Thandi pulled away as though she'd had an electric shock: 'What was that for?'

Sam made a joke of it. He held up his right fist and said, 'Unity is power.'

That was the only time.

Thandi began to go to meetings of student activists. As the year wore on they were more and more regular. At first she went mostly because Meadowlands Beat played their drums at these occasions when the talking was done and the throng fired up and ready to dance. But she was soon impressed by the student leaders and what she considered the ineffable right of their cause. At the end of every speech, the speaker would bellow from the depths of their being, 'Power!' And their audience would answer with one voice, 'To the people!' At the end of every meeting, the leaders would begin a chorus of 'What have we done?' and that phrase would be repeated over and over until it became an indisputable call to arms. Thandi, for one, believed that she was part of a generation on the cusp of something better.

By the middle of the year there were plans afoot for direct action that would force the government to listen. There would be a march, a peaceful demonstration that would close every school for one day.

She considered telling her parents. She briefly thought that her father would be proud but then she realised that he'd probably try and stop her. The older generation had had their chance.

There were few pupils at Thandi's school who knew about it. She and Sam were the main activists so their job was to ensure that their peers joined the occasion. She was certain they would, whether from a desire to protest or simply a desire for an impromptu holiday. Sure enough, when Sam beat his drum in the yard at breaktime and they announced the plan, it was barely ten minutes before they had the whole school behind them.

They marched *en masse* to the agreed meeting point near Orlando Stadium but, with everyone laughing and joking, it was less like a demonstration than a day out. Sam and Thandi were at the front, side by side. He held her hand.

By the time they arrived at the Municipal Hall, it felt like dozens of schools were already gathered and thousands of pupils were already there. The atmosphere was one of barely contained excitement. Then, one of the student leaders climbed up on a tractor and made a speech. 'Brothers and sisters,' he began. 'I appeal to you: keep calm and cool. We have just received a report that the police are coming. Don't taunt them. Don't do anything to them. We are not fighting.'

When the march eventually progressed, there was still some singing, laughing and dancing but the mood was markedly more restrained.

Thandi and Sam were close to the front when the demonstration met the police line. There was a moment's stand-off, a moment's stillness, a moment of uncertainty when nobody – law enforcers and students alike – knew quite what to do next. Thandi saw a policeman spit into the dirt. She spotted another whose hand, she was sure, was shaking on the butt of his gun. An officer made an announcement, something about dispersing, but his loudhailer was drowned in the hubbub. Some of the children were still singing. Some were still laughing. Some were still dancing. Thandi and Sam were still. She could feel his fingers entwined with her own. They were cold.

Then, suddenly, the first gas canister flew. Suddenly there was chaos. Suddenly there was the crack of a gun and suddenly a child fell dead next to them. Sam squeezed Thandi's hand tight and he ran, dragging her after him.

God knows where they ran or how long they ran for. Their eyes were stinging and their lungs ready to burst. They twisted this way and that, they heard screams and gunshots, they ducked down an alley. When they reached the dead end at a corrugated iron fence, they clung to each other. She shook and sobbed and squeezed her eyes tight shut but he was as solid as a tree trunk.

When Thandi opened her eyes, she saw two policemen walking towards them from the top of the alley, their guns drawn. One of them had a moustache. He barked an order at them but Thandi couldn't understand it with the fear in his voice and the strength of his accent. She looked up at Sam. His face was locked in the same expression of seriousness he adopted when drumming. He held her tight for a moment before letting her go for the last time. The policemen had both raised their guns. Sam looked into her eyes and said, 'I noticed you first.' Then he turned and began to hum a tune and quietly tap out a rhythm on the corrugated iron fence.

It took Thandi a moment to catch it but as soon as she did she began to sing. It was an old song, a song from a previous generation of protest, and between her sobs she sang it at the top of her voice. 'Watch out, Verwoerd,' she sang. 'The blacks will get you.'

Sometimes Miss T thinks she can see everything. As she stumbles out into the road, towards the BMW, she sees the arrogance of youth in the gangster who confronts Mama Sylvia and the desperate fear of age in the old woman. But she makes no judgements. She also hears the voice of the young man who has recognised her shouting to his fellows, 'Shut up! Don't you know who that is? It is Comrade Thandi.' But she doesn't listen.

Sometimes Miss T thinks that since her heart was broken open, her weightless soul can escape and look down on her country like a bird and look down on her history like a spirit. And right now she feels like she is flying high and she can see everything.

She can see the whole of Soweto. She can see the route of the march from Meadowlands past Dube Village to Orlando West. She can see the municipal beer halls, including the one where her father used to drink, as they blazed, sacked and looted, for the two days after the June 16th uprising. She can see the point where Sam fell and hear her own wailing as she was hauled away from his fallen body and bundled into the back of an armoured truck.

Now her soul is higher still and in the distance she can see Angola where she trained with MK. Before she was nineteen, she had returned as an intelligence expert at the head of one of the Johannesburg cadres. She can see the police headquarters at John Vorster Square where she was taken on her eventual arrest at twenty-two and the very cell in which she took the beating that cost her an eye. She can see the maximum security prison where she spent the next ten years and she relives the last manacled shuffle of all her comrades who went, some bravely and some less so, to the gallows. She can even see the funeral of her mother and then her father six months later although, of course, she wasn't there for either.

By the time Miss T reaches the group that is gathered around the BMW, she is almost bent double. The pain in her back is so bad that she can't walk far these days and she is looking only at the dust beneath her feet. Suddenly nobody is speaking; the gangsters, Sylvia, the schoolchildren all respectfully quiet. Only the rough beat of the pop music punctuates the silence.

The young man who recognised her has his head bowed and he mumbles, low and ashamed, 'I'm sorry, Comrade Thandi.' Several of the others do the same.

But Miss T doesn't hear them. Instead she hears only the music for there is no better source of empathy. It carries her weightless soul out of her broken heart and back across decades to a schoolyard not far from here where Meadowlands Beat used to play for the joy of it, led by a serious young man called Sam. And now, painfully at first but then joyful and abandoned and intense, Miss T starts to dance.

AUTHOR BIOGRAPHIES

Stella Duffy has written nine novels, the latest of which is *Parallel Lies* (Virago). Her previous novel, *State of Happiness* (Virago), was long-listed for the 2004 Orange Prize. With Lauren Henderson she co-edited the anthology *Tart Noir*, which includes her story 'Martha Grace', winner of the CWA Short Story Dagger in 2002. Stella has written over twenty short stories and many feature articles. She also writes for radio and theatre; with the National Youth Theatre she adapted her novel *Immaculate Conceit* for the Lyric Theatre Hammersmith. In addition to her writing work, Stella is an actor, comedian and improviser.

Mike Gayle is the author of four bestsellers, *My Legendary Girlfriend*, *Mr Commitment*, *Turning Thirty* and *Dinner For Two* (all published by Hodder and Stoughton) which have all at various times lodged themselves in the *Sunday Times* Top Ten. His new book, *His 'n' Hers*, is out now and he's currently working on another, tentatively titled *Brand New Friend*.

So far, **Annabel Giles** has been a model, TV and radio presenter, actress and comedienne. Highlights from those careers include an exclusive contract with Max Factor, not receiving a Gotcha! Oscar from Noel Edmonds, being a regular reporter on Radio Four's *Loose Ends*, starring in several pantomimes and two one-woman sell-out shows at the Edinburgh Festival. She is now an author – her first novel, *Birthday Girls*, was published by Penguin in 2000. She is currently writing her third book, *The Defrosting of Charlotte Small*, which will be available in 2005. Annabel lives with her children in London.

Val McDermid grew up in a mining community in Fife. In a previous life she was a tabloid journalist but has been a full-time writer since 1991. International bestsellers, her books have won awards in the UK, the US and France, including the Gold Dagger, the *Los Angeles Times* Book Award and the Grand Prix des Romans d'Aventure. She has published nineteen novels, a short story collection and one non-fiction book. She has adapted her work for radio and the award-winning TV series, *Wire in the Blood*, is based on her books. She is a regular contributor to BBC Radio.

Shelley Silas was born in Calcutta and grew up in north London. Her plays include *Calcutta Kosher* (Kali Theatre), Southwark Playhouse, UK tour, Theatre Royal Stratford East, *Falling*, The Bush Theatre (Pearson writer-in-residence

2002) and *Shrapnel* (Steam Industry) BAC. Her plays for Radio Four include *INK, Collective Fascination, The Sound of Silence* and *Calcutta Kosher*. She also devised and co-wrote a series of ten short plays, *The Magpie Stories*, adapted Hanan al-Shaykh's novel *Only in London* and co-adapted (with John Harvey) Paul Scott's *The Raj Quartet*. Her new play for Clean Break, *Mercy Fine*, premiered at The Door, Birmingham Rep in October, and opens at the Southwark Playhouse in London in November 2005.

Sophie Kinsella is the author of *Can You Keep A Secret?, The Secret Dreamworld of a Shopaholic, Shopaholic Abroad, Shopaholic Ties The Knot* and *Shopaholic & Sister*. She lives in London with her husband and two sons.

Helen Cross's stories have appeared in various magazines and anthologies, and her plays have been broadcast on the radio. Her first novel, *My Summer of Love*, won a Betty Trask award and was made into a film. Her second novel, *The Secrets She Keeps*, will be published by Bloomsbury in spring 2005.

Born in 1964, **Ben Richards** lives in London. He has been a lecturer in Development Studies at the University of Birmingham and UCL and is the author of five novels, the last of which, *The Mermaid and the Drunks*, came out in paperback this year. He has also written extensively for television, including episodes of the BBC's hit drama *Spooks* and Channel Four's *No Angels*.

Lauren Henderson was born in London, where she worked as a journalist before moving to Tuscany to start writing books. She now lives in Manhattan. She has written seven books in her Sam Jones mystery series: *Dead White Female*, *Too Many Blondes*, *Black Rubber Dress*, *Freeze My Margarita*, *Strawberry Tattoo*, *Chained!* and *Pretty Boy*. The Sam novels have been optioned for a movie deal and translated into fifteen languages. She has also written three romantic comedies, *My Lurid Past*, *Don't Even Think About It* and *Exes Anonymous*, all published by Time Warner, and a non-fiction book, *Jane Austen's Guide to Dating*. Together with Stella Duffy, she has also edited an anthology of girls-behaving-badly crime stories, *Tart Noir*, and their website is www.tartcity.com.

Jake Arnott was born in 1961 and still lives in the twentieth century. He has written three novels. His first, *The Long Firm*, was adapted as a four-part TV drama for BBC2, broadcast in the summer of 2004. *Ten Lords a-Leaping* is his first published short story and is based on an idea that he nicked from his younger brother. He is currently working on his fourth book, *Johnny Come Home*.

Author Biographies

Matt Whyman is an author and agony uncle for *Bliss* and AOL UK. His novels include *Boy Kills Man*, *Superhuman*, *Columbia Road* and *Man or Mouse*. He has also written several teen advice books.

Patrick Neate is the author of three novels: *Musungu Jim and the Great Chief Tuloko* (which won a Betty Trask award), *Twelve Bar Blues* (which won the Whitbread Novel award) and, most recently, *The London Pigeon Wars*. His latest book is non-fiction: *Where You're At: Notes from the Frontline of a Hip Hop Planet* is an investigation of the globalisation and appropriation of hip hop. Patrick is also an acclaimed journalist, critic and screenwriter and he has toured nationally and internationally as a spoken word performer.

You can order other Virago titles through our website: *www.virago.co.uk* or by using the order form below

☐	State of Happiness	Stella Duffy	£6.99
☐	Exes Anonymous	Lauren Henderson	£6.99
☐	Don't Even Think About It	Lauren Henderson	£6.99
☐	My Lurid Past	Lauren Henderson	£5.99

The prices shown above are correct at time of going to press. However, the publishers reserve the right to increase prices on covers from those previously advertised, without further notice.

Virago

Please allow for postage and packing: **Free UK delivery.**
Europe: add 25% of retail price; Rest of World: 45% of retail price.

To order any of the above or any other Virago titles, please call our credit card orderline or fill in this coupon and send/fax it to:

Virago, PO Box 121, Kettering, Northants NN14 4ZQ
Fax: 01832 733076   Tel: 01832 737526
Email: aspenhouse@FSBDial.co.uk

☐ I enclose a UK bank cheque made payable to Virago for £ . . . .
☐ Please charge £ . . . . . . to my Visa/Access/Mastercard/Eurocard

☐☐☐☐☐☐☐☐☐☐☐☐☐☐☐☐☐☐

Expiry Date ☐☐☐☐   Switch Issue No. ☐☐

NAME (BLOCK LETTERS please) . . . .

ADDRESS . . . .

. . . .

. . . .

Postcode . . . . Telephone . . . .

Signature . . . .

Please allow 28 days for delivery within the UK. Offer subject to price and availability.

Please do not send any further mailings from companies carefully selected by Virago ☐